HEART TO HEART

By Helen Perelman

Based on the Disney Channel Original Movie
High School Musical, written by Peter Barsocchini

Bath New York Singapore Hong Kong Cologne Delhi Melbourne

First published by Parragon in 2008
Parragon
Queen Street House
4 Queen Street
Bath BA1 1HE, UK

ISBN 978-1-4075-1744-5

Printed in UK

CHAPTER ONE

The East High auditorium was bustling as all the students filed in for the mandatory Monday morning assembly. When Gabriella Montez walked in, there was so much noise she could hardly hear her friend Taylor McKessie.

"What did you say?" Gabriella asked, leaning in closer to Taylor.

"I said," Taylor repeated, a bit louder this time, "I can't believe we're missing chem lab for this." She gave her chemistry textbook a big hug. "I love chem lab."

Gabriella smiled. Most kids at East High were happy to have an assembly get-out-of-class-free card, but Taylor was different. As leader of the East High Scholastic Decathlon team, the girl was obsessed with school, especially science.

"Maybe it won't be the whole period," Gabriella said, trying to reassure her friend.

"Students, please come in and take a seat." Principal Matsui's voice boomed through the speakers. Onstage, the Principal was gesturing for students to come in and sit down. He leaned in closer to the microphone that was perched on the podium. "We'd like to get started."

"Hey, Taylor! Hey, Gabriella!" Martha Cox called from the fifth row. Martha was on the Decathlon team and had saved some seats for them. She moved her bag and jacket, and motioned for them to join her.

"Thanks," Taylor said as she sat down.

"Hi," Gabriella said, though she couldn't help

but be a bit distracted. Where was her friend Troy Bolton? Maybe he had thought to save her a seat, too? She didn't get to see him before registration, and she was anxious to talk to him. They had talked on the phone the night before, but she always felt like she had so much to tell him.

"Good morning, students," Principal Matsui said.

The audience quietened down as everyone finally slid into their seats.

"It is my pleasure to welcome you to this special assembly about our participation in the United Heart Association Valentine's Day Challenge."

"Valentine's Day *is* a challenge!" someone from the crowd called out.

A roar of laughter came from the back of the auditorium.

Gabriella turned around. She thought it sounded like a comment Chad Danforth would make. Not only was he a great basketball player, but he was also a jokester. In the back rows of the auditorium she spotted Chad, laughing with his basketball-team buddies. Troy was sitting next to him. Just as she was about to turn back to face the stage, Troy caught her eye. Gabriella blushed and gave a small wave. Troy nodded and flashed her one of his dazzling smiles.

Chad's joke got the room buzzing, and Principal Matsui tried to quieten the crowd once again. He leaned closer to the microphone. "Heart to Heart is an annual fundraiser and an excellent cause. You can all make a difference."

Gabriella turned to look back at Troy again. He was playing with the string from the hood on his sweatshirt. Gabriella smiled. Maybe this year Valentine's Day will be a little different, she thought as she settled back into her seat. As she turned her eyes once again to the front of the auditorium, she wondered if Troy was thinking the same thing.

Principal Matsui was still speaking to the assembly. "This year, Sharpay Evans will be the Captain of the event. She will let you know all the details. Please welcome her to the stage."

Sharpay walked up the steps to the stage as if she were at the Academy Awards® in a beautiful ballgown. She took her time strutting up to the podium where Principal Matsui was standing. In her red, velvet blazer and tailored white wool trousers, she looked like a Valentine's Day art project.

"Hello, East High!" she greeted the crowd, turning on her charm full blast.

Ryan, Sharpay's brother and singing partner, and the Drama Club Co-President, was sitting in the front row. He jumped up and gave a huge *whoop*! He then looked down the row at some of the other drama club members to follow his lead. A few clapped lightly.

"It is a pleasure to be here today," Sharpay said clearly and slowly. She was used to being onstage in front of the whole school. After all, she was the Co-President of the drama club and the lead in most shows. Centre stage was her home.

She looked down at the pink note cards that she had carefully prepared the night before. Being the Captain of Heart to Heart was a huge responsibility and a big honour.

"Our goal this year is to raise the most money in the county for the United Heart Association. I have devised a plan to help us reach our goal." Sharpay looked up at her audience and gave them another huge smile. "Each school club will create a fundraiser for the week of Valentine's Day. If we all work together, we can beat West High!"

Principal Matsui cleared his throat and stepped forward.

"I mean, we can raise a lot of money for the United Heart Association," Sharpay said. She couldn't help but mention West High. Their rival high school had won the challenge five years in a row. Now that Sharpay was the Captain of the event, she was determined that East High would win.

"The drama club will be running the annual

flower delivery to form rooms on Valentine's Day. Forms will be available beginning on Monday." Sharpay paused and looked at her classmates. "Now remember, Wildcats, next Friday is Valentine's Day!"

"And not only that, we've got a game against South High!" Chad bellowed from the back. The students all cheered.

Sharpay smiled and held up her hand for quiet. "With the help of my drama club friends," Sharpay said, "we'd like to present, 'Flowers'. It's a little song that we came up with to express our feelings about the event."

On Sharpay's cue, Kelsi Nielsen, East High's most talented pianist and composer, entered from stage right pushing a piano. Ryan leaped up from his seat to join Sharpay on the stage. They had rehearsed this song and dance numerous times. Ryan loved the song. And clearly, he loved any chance to sing and dance.

Kelsi started to play the opening chords while Sharpay and Ryan moved the podium off to the side. They always liked to be in the middle of the stage for their routines.

Ryan got into position next to his sister and gave the audience a smile. Then he tilted his red cap forward over his eyes.

"How do you say you're special to a friend? What gives you the power?" Sharpay sang.

"A *flower!"* Ryan sang out in response.

"Yes," Sharpay bellowed in perfect pitch. *"Send a flower and make a donation to the United Heart. You'll be doing your part!"*

Gabriella turned around to look at Troy. He rolled his eyes and put his hands over his ears to block out the goofy song.

The performance had a big finish, with a short tap dance followed by a flip. Ryan and Sharpay held the last pose, waiting for applause. There were a few claps – mostly from the other drama club members sitting in the front row. And, of course, Ms Darbus, the drama teacher, always appreciated a good song-and-dance routine, so she joined in, clapping as loudly as she could.

But there were mostly moans from the rest of the audience.

"Oh, brother," Taylor whispered to Gabriella.

"Oh, brother and sister!" Gabriella said with a giggle.

"They need some new moves," mumbled Martha. She was very into hip-hop and was a great dancer herself.

Principal Matsui returned to the podium and took the microphone in his hands. "Thank you, Sharpay, Ryan and Kelsi, for that interpretive routine," he said. "I hope that all of you will think about how you can contribute to this special school event."

The bell rang, and the students started to head out of the auditorium.

"Please report to your third-period class," the Principal announced. "There will be a sign-up sheet outside the front office. I encourage every club to participate in this challenge. Thank you, East High!"

Taylor grabbed her backpack and stood up.

"Sharpay thinks that this is all about her. Well, this year, the Scholastic Decathlon team is going to raise the most money for the United Heart Association. I'm glad that we have a meeting today after school."

Gabriella raised an eyebrow. The Decathlon team was filled with some great people who knew lots of facts and figures. But what did they know about romance and Valentine's Day?

"Okay, guys," Taylor said, addressing the Decathlon team after school. "We can do this. We just need to think of one great idea."

The team was gathered in a classroom to discuss their fundraiser for Heart to Heart. The buzz in the hallways all day was about the upcoming challenge.

"We're scientific people," Taylor told them. She looked at each one of her team-mates sitting at the table. "We can apply logic and brainpower to this problem. We will use proven scientific principles as our guide."

"Love is not scientific," Martha said.

The others nodded in agreement.

"We can come up with a good idea," Taylor said. "It's not like the only way to raise money is by delivering flowers." She got up and walked around the room.

"Well, giving flowers on Valentine's Day is an ancient tradition," offered Timothy Martin, a member of the team. "There's a long history of exchanging agricultural products as part of mating rituals."

"He has a point," Gabriella said. She didn't want to see Taylor upset, but she had to admit that Sharpay had secured the best idea for the Heart to Heart Challenge. They would have to think hard about creating another activity that would raise as much money.

"Maybe we should think outside the box," Martha said. She powered up her laptop. "Let's do some research on the history of Valentine's Day."

Soon the group was reviewing pages of

information that Martha printed from the Internet. Gabriella stood back and looked at a list of facts about the romantic holiday. But she was distracted, thinking about what this Valentine's Day would mean for *her*. Should she buy Troy a Valentine's Day gift? she wondered. What should she get him?

Taylor walked over to the blackboard. "History isn't helping," she said. She took a piece of chalk in her hand. "Let's try to work this out mathematically. If Z equals love and Y equals Valentine's Day," she said, writing the equation on the board. "Then all we need to do is solve the equation for X. So clearly the problem is as simple as X equals Z minus Y!"

"The question is, what is X?" Martha said.

"And how much can we charge for it?" Taylor added.

"Is anyone else hungry?" Timothy moaned.

Gabriella smiled at Timothy. Then she said, "My mum always says the best way to a man's heart is through his stomach."

Taylor's face lit up. "That's it!" She rushed over to Gabriella and gave her a huge hug. "Oh, Gabriella," she gushed, "you are brilliant! You are absolutely brilliant!"

Gabriella smiled, but she was wondering what she had said that had got Taylor so enthused.

CHAPTER TWO

"**K**eep it going!" Coach Bolton yelled. "Move the ball. Let's go!"

The basketball team was hustling down the court doing drills. With the big game coming up the following week, Coach Bolton was extra serious about fundamentals and stamina. And lately, that meant the team was going through some tough practices.

"Good pass, Zeke!" Coach Bolton called. He gave a thumbs-up to Zeke Baylor after his passing sprint. "Look alive, Chad!"

Chad was behind Zeke, and he was exhausted. This was their fifth drill and he was beginning to feel as if his trainers had turned to lead.

"Dude, he is on a rampage," Chad whispered to Troy as they reached the foul line. "This drill is killing me."

"I know," Troy said. "He's really focused on getting us in top shape for the game next week."

"We have to beat South High," Jason Cross said as he came up behind Chad and Troy. "That's huge."

"Man, I know," Troy said.

"But I don't think I can take much more of this," Chad complained.

"Chad, you're next!" Coach Bolton's voice broke up the conversation. "Heads up. Move those feet."

Chad ran down the court, passing and dribbling the ball back and forth to Troy. They had a great rhythm together and made it down to the basket at the other end of the court without missing a step.

"Good work!" Coach Bolton cheered.

Troy smiled. He knew that the game next Friday was a big deal for the team – and for his dad. Having his father as his coach was hard at times, but Troy had seen lots of other coaches and thought that his dad was the best. When it came to basketball, Troy liked things to be the best that they could be.

"Okay, guys!" Coach yelled. "Full-court sprints. Let's move it."

The team organized into two lines and took turns running in pairs down the court and back.

"Hey, Troy," Zeke said as he waited his turn. "Did Sharpay talk to you? She keeps asking what the team is going to do for the fundraiser."

"I know," Troy replied. "I've been avoiding her all day. She's on a mission, that's for sure."

"You know the ladies get all crazy about the big V-day," Chad said. He made a swooning face, clasping his hands under his chin.

Jason laughed and gave Chad a shove.

"Hey, nothing wrong with celebrating Valentine's Day," Zeke said. "I love the day. I'm making a chocolate soufflé for my mum. It's a tradition."

Troy smiled at Zeke. "Save me a piece, dude, and I'll be your valentine!"

"Chad! Troy! You're up," Coach called. "No slackers. No turtles. Let's keep it moving."

Troy took off. He knew that as Team Captain, he had to think of ideas for the fundraiser. But all he could think of now was Gabriella. As his feet pounded the floor, he tried to think what would be the perfect gift for her. Maybe she would like a drama-club flower? Was that lame? Or maybe he could think of something really cool for them to do together. Suddenly, Troy wanted to make this Valentine's Day really special for her.

Troy and Chad reached the foul line at the same time. They high-fived each other and leaned against the red pads on the gym wall to catch their breath.

"You're thinking about Gabriella, aren't you?" Chad asked. He could recognize that look in his friend's eye. It was a look that Chad had come to see quite often.

Troy shrugged. He looked around to make sure that the other guys didn't hear him. He leaned in to confide in his friend. "I don't know what to do about Valentine's Day. I'm not even sure what Gabriella expects."

Chad slapped his buddy on the back. "She expects a gift, dude."

This didn't make Troy feel any better. The pressure was starting to build. And unlike basketball, he didn't have a game plan.

"But first, you gotta think of a team fund-raiser," Chad told him. He pulled his leg up to stretch his quad muscle. "The basketball team has to come up with a good one, one that raises the most money." Chad switched legs. "Plus, you don't want to endure the wrath of Sharpay."

Jason finished his sprint and walked over to them. "I say we don't do anything."

"Oh, that's brilliant," Troy said with a laugh. "No way will Sharpay allow that on her watch."

Jason shrugged. "I guess not, but when do we have time?" Then he thought of an idea. "How about we sell tickets to watch us practise?"

"Oh, that's a super-fun idea," Zeke said, giving Jason a playful jab in the arm.

"Valentine's Day is not meant to be fun," Chad told him.

Troy looked at his buddies. That wasn't cool. The United Heart Association was a really good cause. "Come on, guys. We can think of something that's fun."

"Okay, team," Coach Bolton said. He blew his whistle and everyone gathered around him. "We have a week before the game, and I want us all to focus. We need to stay on top of our drills and really concentrate on the fundamentals." He looked around at all the players. "Let's make each practice count. We have an excellent shot at clinching the conference title. But first we have to beat the South High Tigers on Friday. They're a tough team. I am going to need you to put all your energies into this game."

The team nodded. Winning the game against the Tigers would be huge for both the school and the team.

"We can do this!" Troy cheered. He caught his father's eye and smiled. His dad gave him a huge grin.

"Go, Wildcats!" Chad cheered.

The team responded with a roar. Troy smiled. He loved basketball, he loved his team and he loved being the Captain. He had a good feeling about next week's game. He was sure they were going to beat the Tigers. It was their time. Now *that* was something to think about.

In the locker room, there was more discussion about the Heart to Heart Challenge.

"I'm open to suggestions about the fundraiser," Troy said to the team. He hoped that together they could come up with something fun and original for the event.

Zeke sat on a bench in front of Troy. "Sharpay

is already on the warpath. In maths class she kept passing me notes asking about the team's idea."

"Like I said before," Jason told the group, "Coach has planned a practice every day after school. And the game is Friday, on Valentine's Day."

The team nodded in agreement. Everyone looked a bit deflated.

"Troy's on it," Chad said, trying to raise morale. "He isn't our Captain for nothing. He'll think of something cool."

Everyone on the team looked at Troy.

I can't even think of something to get for Gabriella, Troy thought. How am I going to come up with a fundraiser that requires no time and fits in with our practice schedule?

But he was the Captain of the team, and right now everyone was waiting for him to speak.

"Don't worry, guys," he said, looking around at his team-mates. "We'll think of something."

In the prop room backstage, Sharpay was barking orders to Ryan and Kelsi. She was intent on making the drama department's flower drive the most profitable fundraiser in the school. She wasn't Captain of Heart to Heart for nothing.

"Make sure that those red ribbons are all exactly 12 inches," Sharpay said to Kelsi, who was cutting the ribbons and placing them in a box. "When we get the delivery on Thursday, we'll have to wrap the flowers and attach the messages."

Ryan was sitting next to Kelsi. He was humming 'Flowers', the song from the morning assembly. It was a pretty catchy tune. He looked up at his sister. "This morning was great, don't you think, Sharpay?"

Sharpay touched her perfectly styled blonde hair. "Yes, it was pretty terrific." She grinned.

At that moment, Sharpay's mobile phone rang. She ran to her bag and searched for her pink phone. "*Helloooo*," she sang into the phone.

Kelsi looked up at Sharpay. Did Sharpay always think that she was onstage? She watched as the Drama Club Co-President paced around the room, flipping through pages on her clip-board.

"Okay, yes," Sharpay said into the phone. "Yes, we need all of those for Thursday after-noon. Thank you! Bye!"

"Who was that?" Ryan asked. He had finished with the red ribbon and reached for the pink rib-bon roll.

"That was the florist. I was confirming the order for next week," Sharpay said as she marked a paper on her clipboard.

"How can you confirm an order when we haven't started selling the flowers yet?" Kelsi asked.

As soon as she asked the question, she real-ized that she shouldn't have doubted Sharpay. There was a moment of silence as Sharpay glared at Kelsi through narrowed eyes.

"We will sell all those flowers," she said in a loud voice. "Don't think for a minute that this will not be the best flower drive that East High has ever seen!"

Kelsi nodded and went back to cutting the ribbons. She was not a huge fan of Valentine's Day. And she didn't like all the attention the holiday was getting at East High. All anyone was talking about in the halls today were Valentine's Day plans. Kelsi was happy to help out with the fund-raiser for the United Heart Association, which was why she agreed to cut ribbon with Sharpay and Ryan after school. But working *with* Sharpay usually meant working *for* her. And Sharpay didn't like anyone questioning her direction.

"Ryan, did you pick up those order forms?" Sharpay asked. She was still looking at her to-do list on the top of her clipboard. "The copy centre was supposed to have them ready after school."

"I did pick them up," Ryan said. He pointed to the four large boxes sitting in a corner. "I almost broke my back getting them here. How many forms did you order?"

"Well, we need to make sure those forms are everywhere," Sharpay told Ryan. Then she looked at Kelsi. "That is our top priority!"

Kelsi nodded and snipped more ribbons.

At that moment, Ms Darbus came into the prop room.

"Hello, students!" she said. She smiled at her star pupils. "What are we creating here?"

Sharpay replied with a smile. "We're cutting ribbon for the Valentine's Day flowers. Every flower will have a ribbon and a message."

"That's very nice," Ms Darbus said. She watched as Kelsi and Ryan cut ribbon and Sharpay sat on a stool going through her papers. Ms Darbus raised one eye and considered Sharpay. She wasn't sure what Sharpay was so busy with, but she trusted that Sharpay would get the job done. "Well, good luck," Ms Darbus said. "It should be a romantic week."

"Oh, goodie," Kelsi mumbled. She was not one for celebrating the holiday.

"Oh, come on, Kelsi," Ms Darbus said. "Next week is Valentine's Day week . . . don't be grouchy."

Kelsi gave her a small smile.

"You never know who might send you a flower," Ms Darbus told her. "Oh, I do love Valentine's Day . . . and flowers. It is all so magical! It will be so much fun."

"Oh, Ms Darbus," Ryan cooed. "You are a big romantic, aren't you?"

Ms Darbus laughed. "Oh, my dear," she said, "we all could do with a little romance."

"That's right," Sharpay agreed. "And this year, everyone at East High is going to get into the spirit."

"Have fun, kids!" Ms Darbus said as she walked out of the prop room. "Don't stay too late and remember to turn off the lights."

Ryan looked up from his work. "Hey Sharpay, I have a great idea! Why don't we deliver the flowers with a song? You know, like a singing telegram?"

Sharpay thought for a moment about her brother's suggestion. "Interesting idea, Ryan," she said. "But it would be impossible for us to go to every form room and sing. There are just too many classrooms."

"Hmm, I guess you're right," Ryan replied. He continued cutting and started to hum 'Flowers' once again.

Kelsi rolled her eyes. Sharpay didn't even consider that someone other than her and Ryan could deliver the flowers with a song. The school chorus – and the whole drama club – could carry a tune. But she didn't dare question Sharpay twice.

Sharpay looked at her list and sighed. "Isn't this going to be splendid? We are going to spread love and joy throughout the school. The drama club always has the best fundraisers. And now all my adoring fans will have an opportunity to send me flowers while raising money for a great cause. It's all so perfect!"

"If you want to beat West High, you have to get the whole school to work together," Kelsi said. "Just selling the flowers isn't enough. Last year, West High broke their own record for the amount of money they raised." She looked up at Sharpay and Ryan as she cut her last ribbon piece. Both of them were just staring at her.

"Kelsi's right, of course," Sharpay said, standing up. She straightened her red jacket and smoothed her white trousers. "That is why it is very important to make sure that all the clubs participate."

"Sure," Ryan said. He was trying to be supportive. "But we have the best fundraiser. The drama club always raises the most money."

Sharpay's mobile phone rang again, and she grabbed it before the second ring.

"*Helloooo*," she sang into the phone happily.

Kelsi witnessed Sharpay's face change from a smile to a pinched frown. This clearly was not someone Sharpay wanted to talk to right now. She watched as Sharpay drew her breath in and then let out a long exhale.

"Well, best of luck to you, too," Sharpay said.

As she punched her mobile phone off, Ryan looked up at her.

"Who was that?" he asked.

"That was Hilary Lloyd," Sharpay said. "She's from West High. We're co-chairs of the Heart to Heart event. We have to get all the schools in the area involved and go to meetings with the United Heart Association programme director." Sharpay tossed her head to the side. "She thinks that West High has this challenge all sealed. Well, I am not going to stand by and let that happen. Just because West High has won for the past few years doesn't mean that Hilary Lloyd knows all."

Oh, boy, thought Kelsi. She had seen that look in Sharpay's eyes before. The girl was determined. Was East High ready for this? Were they ready for Sharpay's endless lists on her clipboard? Kelsi sighed. She hoped that everyone at East High would get behind this challenge – or else they might face Sharpay's wrath. But Kelsi had to wonder, did the Wildcats have enough heart?

CHAPTER THREE

When the final bell of the day rang on Friday, Taylor had a huge smile on her face. She was waiting until the Scholastic Decathlon meeting that afternoon to tell the club about her great idea for a fundraiser. Gabriella's comment at Monday's meeting had got her thinking. And now she knew that she had a fantastic plan that would raise a lot of money for the United Heart Association. Taylor was very pleased with herself. She smiled as she walked down the hall.

30

"Hey, Taylor!" Gabriella called. "Wait up!"

Taylor turned to see Gabriella running towards her. She stopped and waited for her.

"So are you finally going to tell me why I'm so brilliant?" Gabriella asked. Ever since the meeting on Monday she had been dying to know what had set Taylor's brain turning. The suspense was killing her.

Taylor threw her arm around her friend's shoulder. "Well, Ms Montez, let's go to the meeting and find out!"

Gabriella shrugged. She had tried all week to get Taylor to let her in on the secret, but Taylor would not crack. She wanted the whole team to find out at once.

For Gabriella, the week had dragged by; she hadn't seen Troy at all outside of school because his father had the team practising every afternoon. She wanted the East High basketball team to beat one of their biggest rivals, but she also wanted to see Troy. They hadn't talked about Valentine's Day yet, but Gabriella was already starting to think of plans. She wanted to make this Valentine's Day really special for Troy. He had been playing so much basketball lately that he didn't have a lot of free time. Valentine's Day would be the first night in weeks that he wouldn't have to think about a practice the next day. If they won the game, it would be a celebration. If they lost, well, Gabriella wanted to be there for him. This made the day even more important to her. She wanted it to be perfect.

Timothy and Martha were already sitting at the table waiting when the girls walked into the room. As Taylor sat down, a few others walked in and took their seats. Gabriella noted that everyone was on time for the meeting. Taylor's secret plan had piqued their curiosity.

"Okay, guys," Taylor began. "I am so glad that you were all able to come to today's meeting. As you know, this year our goal is to raise the most money for the United Heart Association's Heart to Heart fundraiser."

"And to beat West High!" Timothy exclaimed.

The others smiled, but Taylor kept on with her speech.

"So as our esteemed team-mate, Gabriella, noted at the last meeting, the way to a man's heart is through his stomach." Taylor stopped and looked around at the cleverest students at East High. "Or a woman's, I might add," she said with a wink. "We are going to reach all of East High through their stomachs by selling cupcakes that will be delivered in registration on Friday. It's a cupcake-gram!"

Martha jumped up. "That's a great idea, Taylor!"

Timothy nodded. "It is a well-known fact that providing nutrients and calorific input are important to creating the ideal brain chemistry for love."

Taylor smiled in agreement and then looked at Gabriella. She was waiting for her response.

"Who is going to bake all the cupcakes that you are planning to sell?" Gabriella asked. She looked around the room. While everyone there could solve a maths equation or a chemistry problem in record time, she doubted that any one of them could bake a delicious cupcake.

"Well, that part of the equation isn't exactly settled," Taylor said. She looked a little concerned. But then she shot Gabriella a pleading look. "You know who could help us, don't you?"

Gabriella knew that Taylor was thinking of Zeke. Not only was Zeke a great basketball player, but the guy loved to bake. And he was really good. Gabriella had been lucky enough to have tried a few of his recipes. Asking Zeke to help was a great idea . . . though knowing how hard the basketball team was practising, it seemed unlikely that he would have time.

"I was hoping that Gabriella would come with me to ask Zeke," Taylor said. She kept her eyes on Gabriella and smiled. "I figured if the two of us asked him, we'd have a better chance of him saying yes."

The whole team was staring at Gabriella. Gabriella blushed. Now she knew why Taylor hadn't told her of her plan earlier.

"Of course, I will," Gabriella said. "But I'm not sure how much free time Zeke is going to have this weekend and next week. The Wildcats are practising constantly these days."

"Well, we can do the baking," Martha said, "and Zeke can be the executive chef."

Everyone looked a little sceptical.

Martha stood up. "Seriously, guys," she said. "What's a recipe? It's just like a chemistry experiment. We can follow a formula."

"True," Timothy said. "But who is going to buy a Valentine's Day cupcake if they think we cooked it up in chem lab?"

Timothy's comment brought Taylor's mood way down. She noticed that many of her team-mates were also looking doubtful.

"Everyone loves a cupcake," Taylor said. "Marketing is all scientific. We can do this. Remember, it's for a good cause."

Gabriella was impressed with Taylor's ability to turn everyone's opinion around so quickly.

Suddenly the very left-brained science team became right-brained creative artists. Everyone powered up their laptops and loaded up their desktop publishing programs to create flyers and signs to hang in the hallways.

Staring at her blank screen, Gabriella didn't feel inspired. She was too busy thinking of what she could plan for after the game. What could she do that would be a great surprise for Troy? Maybe they could go to dinner? Or was that too boring? Maybe they could listen to some music? As her mind formed more and more questions, she drew hearts around the border of her poster.

"Hey, these flyers are looking pretty good," Taylor said as she picked up some sheets from the printer. "We're going to rule this fundraiser."

"We have a good chance," Timothy said. "But what are we calling these cupcake-grams? I think we need a catchy slogan."

Taylor had thought about that question already. And she was ready with an answer. "These are Love Cakes! Send them to your crush! Send them to a friend! One bite and they'll know how you feel!"

"That is some cupcake!" Martha exclaimed.

"Let's just hope that we can come through on our promise," Gabriella said.

After the Decathlon meeting was over, Gabriella and Taylor walked to the gymnasium. Knowing that the basketball team was probably finishing practice, it seemed like a good bet that they would find Zeke there.

Taylor was still smiling from the Decathlon meeting. The order forms and flyers looked great. She was confident that her club was going to contribute to East High's winning tally for the Heart to Heart fundraiser.

Gabriella was trying to think of what to say to Zeke. They needed his help if they were going to make this idea work. Sure, Love Cakes had potential as a fundraiser, but they had to taste good, too.

"Do you think Zeke will help us?" Taylor asked Gabriella.

"My bet is that he will," Gabriella responded. "He loves to bake. And this is an easy task. The guy makes crème brûlée, and that has to be a hundred times harder than cupcakes."

"Let's hope you're right," Taylor said.

Gabriella shifted her backpack to her left shoulder. There was something else she wanted to ask Taylor. Taylor seemed to be well versed in Valentine's Day etiquette, so she was a good person to talk to. Plus, Taylor was her friend. "Taylor, I want to do something special for Troy for Valentine's Day. Got any ideas?"

Taylor stopped walking. She turned to face Gabriella. "It's Valentine's Day. He should make the plan and get *you* a gift."

"He has been crazy busy with practice and school. I've been thinking that maybe I should be the one to take care of Valentine's Day plans, so he doesn't have something else to worry about," Gabriella confessed. "I just don't know what to do, or what I should get him."

Taylor reached out to grab the large handle

of the gymnasium door. "Hmm. I'm not sure that's the way I'd handle it, but you'll think of something," she told Gabriella. "Right now, we have to see if we can get Zeke to help. Are you ready?"

"Yes," Gabriella said as she followed Taylor into the gym.

The gym was empty. Taylor's smile disappeared.

"They must be in the locker room," Gabriella told Taylor. "Come on, let's go and stand by the door. They walk out over there." She pointed to a door at the far end of the gym.

The girls walked across the empty court. When they got to the centre, Gabriella turned to face the stands. Standing at centre court gave her a little chill.

So this is what it feels like to stand here, she thought. She looked at the basket down one end of the court. It seemed so far away. At that moment, Gabriella had a ton of respect for all the players on the team. And, of course, Troy.

"You're thinking about Troy playing here, aren't you?" Taylor asked. She noted the look in Gabriella's eyes and knew that she was thinking about her valentine.

Gabriella blushed slightly. "Yes, and the other players, too. It's intimidating to stand at centre court. And right now there's no one here. On Friday, this place will be packed with screaming fans. I don't know how they do it."

"We do it because we love the game," Troy said. He walked up behind Gabriella. He had a huge smile on his face. He hadn't expected to see her there. And he was very happy about the surprise.

"Hey, there," Gabriella said, "I didn't see you."

"Hey, there, yourself," Troy said. All week he had tried to catch up with her, but there never seemed to be enough time between classes for them to talk. "It's great to see you."

"It's great to see you, too," Gabriella said. She had a ton of other things that she wanted to tell him. However, all she could do at that moment was smile.

Taylor rolled her eyes. Troy and Gabriella could smile at each other all day. She had to move this along. "Hi, Troy," Taylor said. "Is the rest of the team coming out?"

Troy raised one of his eyebrows. "Who are you looking for, Taylor? Anyone in particular?"

Gabriella giggled when Troy looked at her.

"Actually, yes," Taylor said. "And it's not who you think."

If Taylor was being honest, she would have said that she hoped Chad would be standing at centre court with them. Chad had a way of always making her laugh. But she was here on official business. She was here as the leader of the Scholastic Decathlon team.

"We're here to talk to Zeke," Gabriella said.

"Ah," Troy said with a smile.

At that moment, the doors to the locker room opened and the rest of the basketball team poured out. They were all showered and ready to head home. Gabriella watched the crowd, hoping to see Zeke. He was the last one to leave the locker room.

"Hey, Zeke!" Troy called. "You've got some visitors."

Zeke looked up and ran over to centre court. Not wanting to miss anything, Chad and Jason followed. It wasn't every day that two girls came by for a visit after practice. Clearly, something was going on.

"Hey," Zeke said as he reached centre court. "What's up?"

"I think that these ladies came here to see you," Troy said as he bowed and started to back away.

"Wait!" Gabriella called. "You can stay."

Troy winked at her. "I gotta go. My mum is already waiting outside for me. I'll call you later."

Gabriella couldn't help feeling sad. It was the first time all week that she was able to see Troy instead of just waving to him in the hall between classes. She wanted to run after him. Then she felt Taylor squeeze her arm, and she remembered the reason why they were standing in the gym.

"Hey, Zeke," Gabriella said. "You know about the Valentine's Day fundraiser, right?" She waited for him to nod. "Well, the Scholastic Decathlon team wants to do a cupcake-gram where cupcakes are delivered to your valentine's form room."

"Delicious idea," Chad chimed in.

"Man, I want one," Jason added. "Sign me up for one of those."

"You'll have to hope that someone has a crush on you, Jason," Chad teased.

"Well, that won't be a problem, right, bro?" Jason said, high-fiving Chad. "The ladies love the J-man!"

Taylor was getting a little impatient. She thought that Gabriella was taking too long to ask the big question. She turned to Zeke. "We need someone who knows how to bake," Taylor said. "We have no clue. Can you help us?"

Zeke looked at the girls and then at Chad and Jason. "The leader of the Scholastic Decathlon team is asking for my help?"

"Yes," Taylor said. "You're the best baker I know. We would really love you to help us out."

"So you want me to bake the cupcakes?" Zeke asked.

"Well, we'd do all the work," Gabriella assured him. "We just need someone to give us the recipe and guide us. You know, like be the coach."

"Wow," Zeke said. "That's so cool that you are asking me. I mean a cupcake is pretty basic, but I do have some recipes for some delicious icings and maybe we could even add some filling to the cupcakes."

"That's terrific, Zeke," Gabriella said. "Could you come over sometime early next week? I know you have practice, but maybe just for a little bit?"

"Sure," Zeke said. "I can swing that."

Chad looked at Taylor. "This is a really clever idea. Did you come up with it?"

"Um, yes, I did," Taylor answered, blushing.

"You're way ahead of us," Jason lamented. "We haven't got our act together for a fundraiser idea."

"But we're on it," Chad said, cutting Jason off. "The East High Wildcats are going to come through with a great fundraiser. Not to worry. Our team is going to be part of this, too."

"Perfect," Taylor said. She was impressed that Chad was so behind this fund-raising challenge. Maybe he wasn't all about basketball. The guy had a real heart. Taylor smiled at him.

"You know, I could do edible flowers, if you want," Zeke offered. He was still thinking about all the sugary possibilities. "We could put those on top of each cupcake to give it a real Valentine's Day feel. Or we could do a red-velvet cake, which is red cake with vanilla icing. Those are intense."

Taylor grinned. She knew that she had Zeke locked in. He was the perfect solution for the Decathlon team. This fundraiser was going to be a piece of cake.

CHAPTER FOUR

Sharpay and Ryan arrived at school early on Monday morning to deliver order forms to every classroom.

"Good morning, Mr Matsui!" Sharpay called when she spotted the Principal in the hallway.

Mr Matsui was holding his morning coffee in a red-and-white Wildcats mug. "Well, good morning," he said. "You're both here early."

"It's Valentine's Day week," Sharpay explained. "And we have a lot of work to do."

"I'm glad that you're taking this fundraiser to heart," Mr Matsui said. "I have faith in you. And in all the East High Wildcats." The Principal eyed the wagon that Ryan was pulling. "What's that, Ryan?"

"Oh, these are the order forms for the Valentine's Day flowers," Ryan answered.

"Well, that's ambitious," the Principal said as he regarded the wagon, which contained four large boxes. "Glad to see that you are both on top of this. Make sure to drop off one of those forms at the office." Mr Matsui winked and headed down the hall.

"Come on, Ryan," Sharpay ordered. "We've got work to do."

Before they took a step, Sharpay's mobile phone rang and she quickly grabbed her bag. "*Helloooo*," she sang into the phone.

Ryan watched as Sharpay pinched her lips together. It had to be Hilary Lloyd. Only that West High senior could make Sharpay scowl so quickly.

"Really?" Sharpay said. "That's great."

There was a long pause. Sharpay flipped back her hair and started walking down the hall. Ryan strained and grunted as he pulled the wagon, following Sharpay as closely as he could so he'd be able to hear what she was saying.

"Well, not this time," she said. "This is a different year." She pinched her lips even tighter. "See you at the meeting. Bye." Then she ended the call. She shoved her phone back in her bag and turned to Ryan. "The nerve of that girl! Can you believe that she called to gloat before the week has even started? She's so sure that she's going to win this challenge. Well, I have news for her. This year the Heart to Heart Challenge is going to be different. West High is going to hear East High's roar!"

"Totally!" Ryan exclaimed. He wanted to believe that East High could come together for this. If anyone could motivate the school, it was Sharpay.

"Come on, Ryan," Sharpay said. "We have form rooms to visit." And with that she was off, with Ryan at her heels.

At basketball practice that afternoon, the Wildcats were playing well. Troy felt really good about the team as he watched the players from the sidelines. Even though they all complained about the extra practices during the past week – and over the weekend – the team was pulling together. This was one of their best practice games.

We totally have a chance to beat the Tigers on Friday, Troy thought. But then he looked up and saw one of Sharpay's Heart to Heart flyers stuck on the gym door. He still hadn't thought of a fundraiser idea for the team. He knew that as the Captain, they were waiting for him to come up with an idea. Time was running out. They had to come up with something – or Sharpay would never forgive them!

"Looking good!" Chad called, congratulating

himself. He had just shot a three-pointer and was celebrating. He high-fived Jason and then Zeke out on the court.

"Great shot, Chad!" Troy yelled from the sidelines. He was anxious to get back in the game. He hoped that he'd be subbed in soon.

"Troy, get in there," Coach Bolton said as if he'd read his son's mind. "Let's scrimmage for a few more minutes, and then we'll do some drills."

The team grunted. Playing a game was fun, but doing drills was a lot of work . . . and they were tired.

"Man, he's harsh," Jason said to Troy when he came out to the court.

"All the work is going to pay off," Troy told Jason as he passed the ball. "The team is playing really well. We've got to be on top of our game to have a shot at winning."

The scrimmage went on for a while longer. Finally, the whistle blew and the game was over, but practice wasn't.

"All right, team," Coach Bolton said. "Everyone

grab a skipping rope and head to centre court."

"Oh, man," Chad whined. "Skipping is gonna kill me."

"You'll be fine, superstar," Troy said, poking his friend in the side.

"I don't know," Chad replied. "All this practice is getting to me. Every part of me is tired, even my brain."

"So I guess that you haven't come up with a fundraiser, huh?" Troy asked. He had hoped that his best friend would pull through with a great idea.

"I haven't had time to do anything," Chad confessed. "Maybe some of the other guys have an idea. If we don't come up with one pretty soon, Sharpay is going to hunt us down. I don't know about you, but I've been avoiding her all day."

"We'll think of something," Troy said as he grabbed a skipping rope. Then he noticed the other guys on the team looking over at him. They'd expected him to come up with an idea, and he hadn't. Not only had he not come up with a team fundraiser, he had no time to speak to Gabriella. Usually they would hang out or at least talk on the phone. But this weekend, between practices and homework, he hadn't had any free time at all. And it was getting to him.

I wonder what she's doing after school today, he thought. I hope that she's looking forward to Friday's game . . . and to Valentine's Day. He really wanted to make it a special Valentine's Day for her. Though he had a feeling that finding time between now and Friday to get a gift would be hard.

The team started jumping. The rhythm of the ropes hitting the floor made a funky beat.

"Keep it up!" Coach Bolton yelled. "Just five more minutes. Then you can hit the showers." The Coach ducked inside his office.

"Five minutes?" Zeke said, huffing. "I don't know if my heart can take it."

"Don't be such a whiner," Jason said, speeding up his rope. "You're a heartbreaker, not a heart-stopper."

"Ha, ha," Zeke said. "Very funny."

Troy laughed at his friends. Skipping was hard work. But his dad always said that it was great exercise for the heart. Something in Troy's head clicked.

"I got it!" he yelled. He stopped jumping and swung the rope into one hand.

"What?" Chad asked, stopping his jumps.

The rest of the team took their cues from the Captain and stopped jumping. They crowded around Troy.

"Our fundraiser!" Troy exclaimed. His face was flushed from jumping. "We'll skip and get sponsors!"

"We can make money and get in shape at the same time," Chad said. He totally got Troy's plan and already fully endorsed it. "Brilliant, Troy! We can call it the Big Jump."

"Great idea. Now we just have to get it approved," Troy said. "And get people to sponsor us!"

CHAPTER FIVE

"Oh, my!" Sharpay exclaimed on Tuesday morning, when she saw a man standing at the classroom door with a large bouquet. "Who are those flowers for?" She put her hand to her chest. Her smile was extra-wide.

"I am looking for Sharpay Evans," the delivery man said.

"Yes, that's me," Sharpay responded, waving him over. She took out a pink pen and signed her name on his clipboard. "Thank you so much."

The rest of the class watched as Sharpay unwrapped the flowers. She put the large bouquet on her desk. "Flowers," she said wistfully. "How thoughtful. Who can these be from?" She could feel everyone in the class looking at her. She knew that she had the spotlight. And Sharpay knew how to perform.

She opened the little white card stuck in the arrangement. "To Sharpay, from a secret admirer," she read. Then she looked around at her classmates. "Don't you just love getting flowers from a secret admirer?"

Ms Darbus rushed over to Sharpay's desk. "Why, Sharpay, how nice for you! This seems to set up the week of romance, doesn't it?"

Some of the students in the back row moaned.

"Now, class," Ms Darbus said. "Valentine's Day is the perfect time to think about all the great romances in theatre. Let's all pick one of our favourites and rehearse a scene for Friday. I think that will put us all in the mood."

Sharpay glanced around the room. Everyone

was staring at her flowers. She was pleased.

As Gabriella gazed at the huge bouquet sitting on Sharpay's desk, she wondered if she would get anything delivered on Friday morning. She knew that Troy was all about basketball, especially this week. But would he forget about Valentine's Day?

Despite what Taylor had said, Gabriella decided that she was going to handle plans for Valentine's Day. She wanted Troy to know that she was thinking of him.

At the end of class, Sharpay handed out flower order forms. The orders were coming in slowly, and they were not up to the numbers she had hoped. She had to get busy. Most of the clubs had come up with some good ideas for raising money. The photo club was offering portraits, the art club was selling temporary tattoos and the football team was advertising bear hugs. Only the basketball team had not signed the sheet in the office, and they were a big part of her plan. They were the best team at East High, and if she got them involved, more students would get excited about the fundraiser . . . especially during the big pep rally on Friday. Sharpay had to find Troy.

Soon, the bell rang and class was dismissed. The hallway was jammed with students. Sharpay navigated through the crowd. She knew what route Troy took to get to maths class. She planned to intercept him and get him to commit to Heart to Heart. As she turned the corner, she spotted him.

"Troy!" she called. "I need to talk to you."

Troy spotted Sharpay. He waved and shouted back over the crowd. "Yeah, I'm on it, Sharpay! The team has got a great idea. Sorry that I didn't sign up earlier. I'll sign up before practice this afternoon."

Sharpay smiled. "Great, Troy," she said. "I knew that I could count on you. Just don't forget, you have to sign up before three o'clock. I have to submit our plan to the committee this afternoon."

"You can count on it," Troy said. He ducked into class just as the second bell rang – and just as Gabriella got to the door.

She had reached the classroom too late. Troy was already in class. Another missed opportunity to talk to him. She'd have to wait until after school, the next chance she would have to see him.

She walked slowly towards the cafeteria. She was meeting Taylor to go over all the ingredients they would need to bake the cupcakes. She had offered up her house after checking with her mum. Mrs Montez was happy to have the Decathlon team over – as long as they promised to leave a few cupcakes behind for her to sample.

When Gabriella entered the cafeteria, she couldn't believe her eyes. The place had been transformed overnight. There was a huge banner reaching across the length of the room advertising Heart to Heart. Little red hearts with people's names on them dangled from the lights. At the far end of the room, there was a table with more hearts. The band was selling the hearts and then hanging them in the cafeteria as their fundraiser. The room was filling up with hearts. Everyone at East High was getting in the spirit.

Gabriella picked up a tray and got in the lunch queue. The queue moved slowly, and she thought about what she would say to Troy when she saw him after school. She decided that maybe she should just come right out and ask him what he thought about Valentine's Day. She would tell him that she would handle all the plans. She sighed. That meant she had to come up with a plan! What could it be?

Taylor was already sitting at a table at the back of the cafeteria. She waved at Gabriella, then moved her books aside, making room for her friend.

"Hi," she said when Gabriella walked over. "Zeke just dropped off the list of ingredients. Here it is." She held up the loose-leaf paper as if it were a precious document. "We can go to the supermarket after school, okay?"

"Sure," Gabriella said, trying to sound enthusiastic. She wanted to be a team player and be part of the baking event, but she also wanted to have time to get Troy a gift and to think about where to go on Valentine's Day.

"What's going on?" Taylor asked. "Did you figure out what you and Troy should do on Friday night?"

Gabriella sank down in the chair next to Taylor. "Not yet. But I'm working on it," she answered. Then she motioned to all the hearts dangling in the cafeteria. "And all this school romance is not making things easier! There's a lot of pressure to think of just the right thing, you know?"

Taylor reached out and put her hand on Gabriella's. "You don't have to worry, Gabriella. Your name is clearly written on Troy's heart."

Gabriella smiled at her friend. Taylor was very clever and often said just the right thing to her.

Gabriella took a bite out of her sandwich. Already she was feeling better.

Then Sharpay appeared at their table.

"Hellooo, ladies," she cooed. "How is everything going? How are the cupcake orders?"

Taylor straightened up a bit. She didn't like having to answer to Sharpay. "We're a little low. But we're going to launch our Love Cakes campaign tomorrow in the morning announcements. Our slogan is, 'Send one to someone you're sweet on'."

"Clever," Sharpay noted. She glanced down at her clipboard. "How much money can I put you down for?"

"A lot," Taylor said, without missing a beat. She was that sure of their plan.

Gabriella did some quick tallying in her head. Clearly, each cupcake order meant that an actual cupcake must be baked. They were promising East High dozens and dozens of cupcakes. That was a lot of baking. She started to get nervous.

Sharpay was pleased with Taylor's response.

"Great news," she said. "I can't wait to see the look on that Hilary Lloyd's face when the East High tally comes in over West High's." Sharpay put her hand on her hip. "She's been calling me all day with updates on how well West High is doing. She's supposed to be helping me organize the United Heart Association meeting on Thursday – not gloating in my face. Can you believe that they are above where they were last year and it's only Tuesday?"

Taylor looked at Gabriella and raised an eyebrow. "Do you think Hilary is telling the truth?" she asked.

"I don't know," Sharpay confessed. "But I can't wait to see that girl's face when we raise the most money."

"We have a good chance," Taylor said.

Gabriella didn't want to be a complete spoil sport, but she was starting to doubt whether it was possible to beat the mighty West High. She kept those thoughts to herself and quietly ate her sandwich.

* * *

Finally, the last bell of the day sounded. Gabriella ran to the gym doors, hoping to see Troy. On her way there, she bumped right into him!

"Hey, there, stranger!" he said. His eyes actually twinkled when he smiled. Gabriella felt her heart leap.

"Hi," she said. "How are you? I can't believe we haven't spoken in so long."

"I know," Troy said. He glanced down at his watch. "I wish I had more time. I really have to go."

"Oh, okay," Gabriella said. She couldn't help but feel a bit blown off. He was heading in the direction opposite the gym. Where was Troy going, and why was he in such a hurry?

"I'll talk to you later!" Troy called over his shoulder. And just like that, he was gone.

Gabriella decided that Troy's behaviour confirmed that he had completely forgotten Friday was anything but a basketball game. Well, she was going to make sure that after the game, he would be pleasantly surprised by her red-hearted plan. She went to find Taylor so they could head to the shop for the cupcake ingredients.

Meanwhile, Troy sprinted down the hall towards the office. He hoped that Gabriella understood he would have loved to stay and hang out with her. But he had to make it to the office before Sharpay's meeting. He had to complete the forms for the basketball team to do their Big Jump for Heart to Heart. But with all his rushing, Troy didn't realize that he hadn't asked Gabriella out for Valentine's Day.

CHAPTER SIX

Kelsi looked at all the piles of paper spread out in front of her. She had stacked the flower orders across the foot of the stage, organized by form. Planning the flower delivery was like orchestrating a huge musical production – it required a ton of planning. Kelsi was actually very pleased with how everything was going. The orders were coming in quickly. She had to hand it to Sharpay, she knew how to motivate the school.

"Hey, Kelsi!" Gabriella called out from the back of the auditorium.

"Oh, hi, Gabriella," Kelsi said. "Are you here to help? I'm almost done arranging all the order forms."

"Wow, you are totally organized!" Gabriella said, impressed. She looked at all the neatly arranged piles on the stage. And then she thought of the forms in her backpack that were all jumbled up. "I just picked up a bunch of cupcake forms from the front office. I'm the one who needs help!"

Kelsi smiled. "You can do it. Just organize the piles by form."

"I guess," Gabriella said. "But we have to bake all the cupcakes, too. I'm a little worried about that."

"Is that all you're worried about?" Kelsi noted. She could tell that something else was bothering her friend.

"Actually, I do have a problem," Gabriella confessed. "I don't know what to do about Valentine's Day."

"That's easy," Kelsi said with a smile. *"Buy him a flower!"* she sang out from Sharpay and Ryan's musical number.

"Ha, ha," Gabriella said. "Seriously, I don't know what to do. I haven't talked to Troy all week. I kind of think he forgot that Friday is Valentine's Day *and* the basketball game. So I decided to plan a special night out."

"Valentine's Day shouldn't be such a big deal," Kelsi said. "But from the amount of these flower orders, it seems people are getting into the spirit. And that's cool." Then she paused. "Though I don't know if we can beat West High. They're much bigger and have this whole fund-raising thing down."

"I know," Gabriella said. "But I'm not going to tell Sharpay that!"

The girls laughed.

"Don't worry too much about Troy," Kelsi said. "You guys are the best couple I know. You don't need a holiday to let each other know that you're good together."

Gabriella smiled. "Thanks." She looked down at her watch. "Oh, I have to run. I'm late to meet Taylor. We have a lot to do! I just came by to see how you were doing." Then Gabriella looked around. "Wait, where's the rest of the drama club? Where are Sharpay and Ryan?"

"Oh, Sharpay will be here any minute to bark out some orders," Kelsi said. She sat down in a chair for a moment and sighed.

"What are you doing?" Sharpay bellowed from the top of the auditorium. She was armed with her pen and clipboard.

Kelsi jumped up out of her seat. It figured that Sharpay would show up just as she sat down, Kelsi thought.

"Everything's all set," Kelsi explained. "Look how many orders we have." She waved her hand up and down the front of the stage.

"Wow," Sharpay said. "This is great." She couldn't believe how many orders there were. "But are we ahead of last year?"

"I don't think so," Ryan said from behind

Sharpay. He walked down the aisle. "I checked the records during my study period. But it's only Wednesday. We still have another day to get orders."

Sharpay looked annoyed. "Where is the romance at East High?"

"I hope that it's not dead," Gabriella mumbled. Then she looked at Kelsi. "I'm going to head out," she told her.

"Well, buy a flower!" Sharpay called as Gabriella raced out of the door.

"I saw Taylor in the hall last period," Kelsi told Sharpay. "She has a huge stack of orders. Love Cakes are going to be huge."

"And the basketball team is doing a skipping event at the pep rally," Sharpay said, tapping her pen on her chin. She consulted her clipboard. "I suppose we have a shot."

"You bet!" Ryan cheered. "Wait until the committee hears how many fundraisers we have going on here."

"Well, we'll see," Sharpay said. She was

dreading the committee meeting that she had to attend with all the local high school liaisons. No doubt Hilary would be bragging the whole time.

"Good luck," Kelsi told Sharpay.

"Thanks," Sharpay replied. "I'm going to need it!"

"Positive energy!" Ryan exclaimed. "Breathe in the good, breathe out the bad." He took a few long, deep breaths in and out.

Sharpay did just as Ryan commanded.

The two of them turned to face each other, doing breathing exercises together for a few minutes. Kelsi rolled her eyes. Sharpay was going to need a lot more than a few deep breaths to get through that cut-throat meeting.

Sharpay walked into West High and headed for the main office. There was a room with a large table where the Heart to Heart committee held meetings. She clasped her clipboard tightly to her chest and entered the room.

"Hello, Sharpay!" Sam Thompson greeted

HSM LOVE LETTERS

East High is a pretty passionate place! Check out the secret notes and steamy Valentines that have been passed in class and hidden in lockers this term - *THEY'RE HOT!*

Dear Gabriella,

If I flunk English, it's all YOUR fault!
I should be paying attention to Ms
Barrington's English class on poetry,
but I can see you sitting at your desk
out of the corner of my eye and you
look so cute, my mind keeps wandering
off. I've been thinking about what an
amazing time we've had together since
you arrived and I can't imagine East
High without you.

TXX

Gabriella

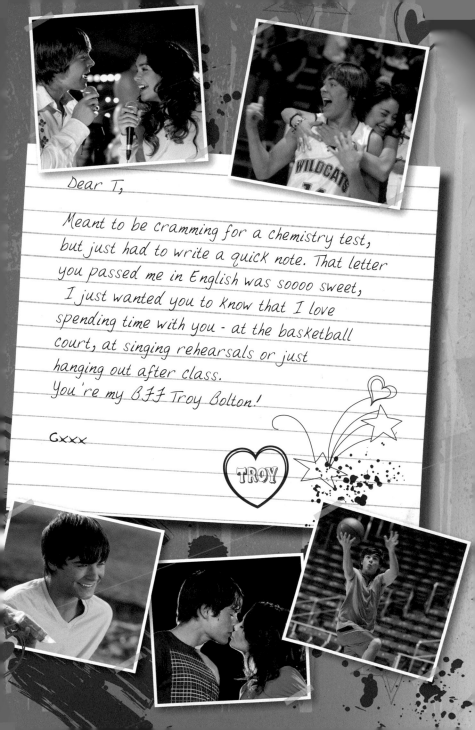

Dear T,

Meant to be cramming for a chemistry test, but just had to write a quick note. That letter you passed me in English was soooo sweet,
    I just wanted you to know that I love spending time with you - at the basketball court, at singing rehearsals or just hanging out after class.
You're my BFF Troy Bolton!

Gxxx

TROY

Sharpay,

Please accept this Chocolate and Passion
Fruit Parfait as a token of my respect.
I've noticed how much you enjoy my
baking and I wanted to create something
dramatic just for you. It's a feather
light sponge, with dark and mysterious
chocolate frosting, topped with exotic
passion fruit.
Hope you like it...

Zeke

P.S Best not to eat it all at once as it
is quite rich.

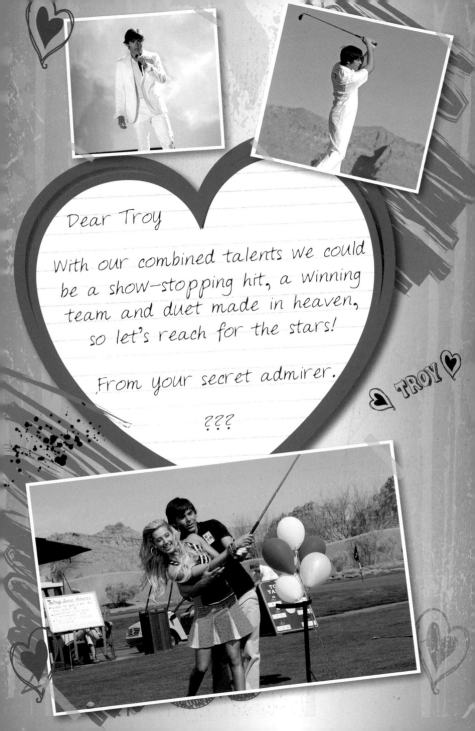

Dear Troy

With our combined talents we could be a show-stopping hit, a winning team and duet made in heaven, so let's reach for the stars!

From your secret admirer.

???

TROY

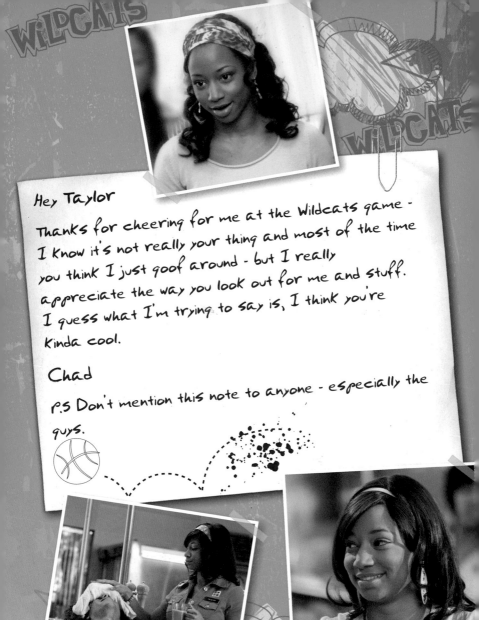

Hey Taylor

Thanks for cheering for me at the Wildcats game - I know it's not really your thing and most of the time you think I just goof around - but I really appreciate the way you look out for me and stuff. I guess what I'm trying to say is, I think you're kinda cool.

Chad

P.S Don't mention this note to anyone - especially the guys.

Hey Chad,

Thanks for the note, although I think it might have been written a while ago — did you have to actually sew it inside the lining of my lab coat?
I know I sometimes get a bit tired of you joking around and hanging with the Wildcats, but I know deep down we've got something good. I guess we just prove the old equation opposite + opposite = attraction.

Taylor
X

Dear Sharpay

I know you probably receive thousands of these every year, but please add this to the pile and BE MY VALENTINE!

I think you are so talented and have such a unique and glamorous sense of style -- you light up the room with your personality.

Your secret admirer

X

her. He was the programme director for the United Heart Association, and he ran the meetings. "We were just waiting for you to get here. Please take a seat." He motioned to an empty chair right next to Hilary.

"Hi, Sharpay!" Hilary sang out.

The meeting had not even started and already Hilary had that smug look on her face.

"Hello, everyone," Sharpay said to the other representatives sitting around the table. She tried to exhale all the bad just like Ryan had said, but it was a little hard sitting right next to Hilary.

"We're going to get started," Sam announced, calling the meeting to order. "I would like to thank you all and your classmates for participating in this year's fundraiser. Thanks to Sharpay and Hilary, we have more schools competing in the challenge than any other year. They have done a super job of involving new schools and making this a real community competition. We appreciate all their hard work."

Sharpay looked over at Hilary, who was

grinning so much it looked like her cheek muscles were about to snap.

"We also need to thank West High," Sam said. He smiled at Hilary. "They have already handed in a cheque for the Heart to Heart Challenge."

The group around the long table all applauded. Hilary stood up and took a bow. She flipped her brown curls to the side and smiled at the committee. Sharpay wanted to scream. The challenge was for the whole week!

"Now, this doesn't mean that the challenge is over," Sam continued. "We hope that every school continues with their plan to raise money. But we are certainly grateful for the early cheque from West High."

Hilary beamed. She was really working the room, nodding and smiling. Sharpay knew what she was up to – and she didn't like it.

"We're doing very well at East High," Sharpay offered up. Everyone at the table looked at her. "Yes," she said. "We have all the clubs involved with several fundraisers going on in school on Friday."

"That's nice," Hilary said. "Of course, *we* always have schoolwide involvement. It's more fun when everyone works together instead of just with their own club."

Sharpay's face was growing hotter and hotter. How dare Hilary think that East High wouldn't come through! East High had heart – and she was going to make sure that everyone on that committee knew it. Especially Hilary Lloyd and West High.

The next morning, Sharpay got to school early once again. She stood on the school steps and addressed East High students as they mingled near the front doors before the first bell.

"Good morning, East High!" she yelled. "You have one more day to make pledges and donations for Heart to Heart. Now is the time! Show the community that East High has heart!"

As she spoke to the crowd, Sharpay felt that she was playing her most important role. East High had the potential to win – they all just had to put a little more heart into the challenge.

"It's Valentine's Day, a day to show the United Heart Association that East High is all about caring. Wildcats, let's see your big hearts!"

As the bell rang and Sharpay walked into the school, she wondered if anyone had heard her.

CHAPTER SEVEN

"**W**here's the sugar?" Taylor cried. She was frantic as she searched Gabriella's kitchen. There were empty boxes everywhere. "Did we run out already? I need one cup."

"I have it," Martha said from across the room. "But we're running low. We'll need to do another supermarket run soon."

Gabriella slumped down on one of the kitchen stools. The Decathlon team had come over after school to bake the Love Cakes. For the last couple of hours, they had been baking like robots. Dozens of cupcakes now lined Gabriella's kitchen and dining room. No one on the team was prepared for the huge orders they had got, but they shouldn't have been surprised. Zeke's recipe for red-velvet cupcakes was amazing. The cake was a combination of vanilla and chocolate, but, with some food colouring, the batter turned a deep ruby-red. The cupcake was then topped with white vanilla icing and red cake decorations.

Zeke had come over the previous night with a sample. "You are totally going to save us," Gabriella told Zeke when she took the box of cupcakes. "We definitely owe you one."

"Well," Zeke replied, "you can sponsor me for the Big Jump at Friday's pep rally." He took out a pledge form from his backpack and handed it to Gabriella.

"Don't worry about that," Gabriella said. "Of course, I'll sponsor you." She took Zeke's form and signed her name. "I'll be at the pep rally to cheer on you and the rest of the basketball team."

"It's gonna be fun," Zeke promised. "Our man Troy totally pulled through with a cool fundraiser. The guy's got heart."

"Yes, he has," Gabriella said, blushing a little.

Then Zeke explained all of the recipe's steps.

"I gave Taylor the list of ingredients. Did you get everything?" Zeke asked.

"Yes, thanks," Gabriella said, licking a little icing off her finger. "I just hope that we can make the cupcakes taste as good as these!" She took a bite out of one of them.

"Make sure you let the cupcakes cool before you ice them," Zeke warned before he left. "And easy on the food colouring, a little goes a long way."

"Thanks again, Zeke!" Gabriella waved goodbye. Then she called Taylor, who came over to taste the treats. That night, both girls knew that they had a winning recipe to get to the heart – and stomach – of every East High Wildcat.

Gabriella smiled. She thought it was going to be so easy but here it was, the day before Valentine's Day, and the Montez kitchen looked like a bakery! Plus, the fundraiser had taken up almost all of her time. The planning, the shopping, the organizing and now the baking, had taken her away from doing anything about a Valentine's Day plan.

"Do you think that we're going to finish baking all this before tomorrow?" Timothy asked. He was surveying the situation in the Montez kitchen and calculating how long each step of the baking took. He scribbled some numbers on a pad and then looked up at Taylor. "I've calculated all the process steps, and at this rate, we will be finishing in twelve thousand, two hundred and twenty-three seconds. We're gonna need an extension."

Taylor exhaled. She had flour on her cheeks

and on her forehead. "There is no extension. Tomorrow is Valentine's Day." Then she looked at everyone in the kitchen. "We can do this," she said, rallying the team. "If we don't produce the cupcakes, we don't get paid. And if we don't get paid, East High doesn't have a chance of winning the challenge."

"She's right," Martha said. She was cracking eggs into a mixing bowl. "Didn't you hear Sharpay before school today? That was some speech she made. I even ended up buying a few extra flowers and hearts. And I'm sponsoring a bunch of basketball players for their Big Jump at the pep rally."

"I know," Timothy said. "I have to hand it to Sharpay, she really spoke from her heart, not from a script."

"Yeah, our cupcake sales got a big boost after she went on and on about being part of the heart of East High," Taylor said. "Now everyone at East High is thinking about Valentine's Day."

"Hello, bakers!" Mrs Montez called as she

walked into the kitchen. "You seem to be pretty busy." She looked at all the empty cartons and flour on the floor. "Um, Gabriella, you are going to clean up this mess, right?"

"Sure, Mum," Gabriella said, jumping off the stool. "Don't worry about it."

"Yes, Mrs Montez," Taylor said. "We'll clean everything. Thank you for letting us use your kitchen."

Mrs Montez smiled at the bakers. "Just make sure that I get at least one of those red-velvet cupcakes. They look delicious!" Then she gave Gabriella a kiss on the head. "I have a dinner meeting, so I'll be home later. Be good!"

Gabriella walked out of the kitchen with her mum. When they were by the front door, Gabriella turned to her. "Mum, I really want to plan something special for Troy for Valentine's Day. He has been practising so much, and I want to surprise him. The thing is, I haven't come up with any ideas yet and tomorrow is Valentine's Day."

Mrs Montez gave Gabriella a hug. "That's very

sweet, honey. I am sure Troy will appreciate you making the plans for the night. Remember, where you go is not as important as who you go with."

Gabriella smiled. "Thanks, Mum. I just want it to be perfect."

"Well, I am sure the night will be," her mum said. "Knowing you and Troy, I bet you'll have a great time. Just think of something that you both love to do." Then she gave Gabriella another kiss and walked out of the door.

As Gabriella stood there, she gave some thought to her mum's advice. And then it came to her! Something that she and Troy both liked to do together was sing! Right next to the supermarket where she and Taylor got all the cupcake ingredients was a new café that offered karaoke. Now *that* sounded like a perfect place to have a Valentine's Day date with Troy.

The buzzer on the oven sounded, and Gabriella ran back into the kitchen. She grabbed an oven glove to fetch the hot tray of cupcakes. "That's another two dozen done!" she cried.

Taylor walked over to her notebook and took out the spreadsheet she had created for the cupcake orders. She studied the paper and then frowned. "We're not even halfway through," she said. "We have a lot more cupcakes to bake."

"And we need to put icing on the ones we have already made," Timothy noted.

"We probably should have started baking before today, huh?" Martha said.

"Most of the orders came in today," Taylor reminded them.

The phone next to Taylor rang.

"Could you get that?" Gabriella asked. She was still holding the hot cupcake tray, searching for a safe place to let it cool.

"Hello, Montez residence," Taylor said into the phone. Then she paused. "Um, actually she's unable to come to the phone."

Gabriella looked up. "Who is it?" she asked.

Taylor covered the mouthpiece. "It's Troy."

Figures, thought Gabriella. She had tried to talk to him all week and the first time he calls, she can't talk to him! "Tell him I can't talk," Gabriella said quickly.

Taylor relayed the message. "No, Troy, she's not mad at you," Taylor said. Then she paused. "At least I don't think so."

Gabriella shot Taylor a look. "Taylor!" she scolded. "Just tell him I'll speak to him later."

Again Taylor spoke into the phone. She nodded her head and then covered the mouthpiece. "He really wants to talk to you."

The tray was getting heavy and was burning her fingers in the glove. She had to set it down. "Just tell him I can't talk!" she called out.

"I think that he heard that," Taylor said. She put the phone back to her ear. "Okay, bye, Troy."

Gabriella finally put the tray down on a rack. She wanted nothing more than to run and call Troy back. But Martha had the batter ready for the next batch of cupcakes. "Well, we better keep moving," Gabriella said. But as she took the bowl from Martha, it slipped out of her hands and sticky red batter splattered everywhere.

"Ouch!" screamed Timothy. In an effort to escape the airborne red batter, he had put his hand down on the hot cupcake tin that Gabriella had just taken out of the oven. He reeled back and bumped into Taylor, who was sifting flour into a bowl. The flour bowl flipped, went flying and landed on Gabriella's head.

"Are you all right?" Taylor said, rushing over to Gabriella.

Gabriella lifted the bowl from her head and tried to brush the flour from her hair. The more she tried to brush it off, the more the white dust seemed to hang on.

"Just perfect," she mumbled. Now Troy thought that she didn't want to talk to him, and a batch of cupcakes were ruined. This was not how she wanted things to go the day before Valentine's Day. Her heart sank as she looked at the huge mess in her kitchen and at her Decathlon team's faces. They were in a serious red-velvet mess.

CHAPTER EIGHT

Troy fell back on his bed and stared at the phone. Then he picked up his basketball and spun it on his finger. As he watched the ball rotate, he wondered what was wrong with Gabriella. She knew that the big game was this week, and that all Troy had been doing was practising. There was nothing new there. He stopped the ball from turning and sat up.

She thinks that I forgot about Valentine's Day, he realized. After all, they hadn't spoken all week, and she was bound to think that he had forgotten. But there was no way he would forget. He had even got her a special gift and thought of a perfect place to take her after the game to celebrate Valentine's Day – and the East High win!

Troy leaped off his bed and grabbed his varsity jacket. He had to go over to Gabriella's house right now. He had to see her and explain.

When Troy arrived at the Montez's front door, he rang the doorbell and waited to see Gabriella.

Taylor answered the door. She had flour on her face and red batter on her clothes. She didn't look like the calm and confident Taylor that Troy knew.

"Troy!" she said, shocked. "I didn't expect to see you. What are you doing here?"

"I came to see Gabriella," Troy said. He peered into the house. "Making cupcakes, huh?" He gave her a smile and walked in. From the sounds and smells, he knew that he'd find Gabriella in the kitchen.

"Troy!" Gabriella cried when she saw him. "You're here!"

"Yes, I am," he said with a wide grin. He looked around the kitchen. There were empty sugar and flour bags on the floor, and Gabriella was on her hands and knees scrubbing up a red glob of batter. "Wow, this is like Grand Central Bakery. How many orders do you guys have?"

Gabriella got up and went over to the counter. Her hair was still streaked with flour. She grabbed Taylor's spreadsheet.

"We're in trouble," she confessed. "It's already after five, and we need to make dozens more – and then ice them all. Martha and Timothy just went to the store for more supplies." Gabriella shrugged. "And we had a bit of a setback before, with a flying batter incident."

"Wow," Troy said, looking at the spreadsheet. "There are a lot of orders. You need to use some teamwork."

"That's what we've been doing," Taylor

snapped as she walked back into the kitchen. "Thanks, Captain."

"No, I mean you need a team . . . a *bigger* team," Troy explained. He took out his mobile phone and punched a few numbers. "And I know just the team to help you."

"Oh, no," Taylor said as she sat down on a stool. "This is going to be bad."

"Hey, man," Troy said into the phone. "Tell the team to meet at Gabriella's for a mandatory practice. Immediately."

Gabriella raised an eyebrow at Troy. When he ended the call, she walked over to him. "It's very nice that you want to help, but I don't see how this would be a mandatory practice for the basketball team."

Troy laughed. "Oh, you can make anything into a basketball drill. Don't worry. The team will be here any minute."

"Wait," Taylor told Troy. "This is the Decathlon's fundraiser and it's our problem. We'll figure out a solution."

"Taylor," Troy said. "This isn't just about the Decathlon team. This is about East High. And the basketball team is East High. We're all in this together."

Gabriella smiled. Troy was right. This wasn't just about each club's fundraiser, the challenge was posed to all of East High. If they came together, they could do this. She reached out to touch Taylor's arm. "Troy's right. We just need a bigger team."

Taylor nodded in agreement. "Okay," she said. "You have a good point."

"Then let's set this place up for some team baking action!" Troy cheered.

Taylor, Troy and Gabriella organized the kitchen so that there were separate stations to mix, cool and decorate the cupcakes. Already Gabriella was feeling better. It was nice to spend time with Troy and to have him on her team.

The doorbell rang, and a bunch of basketball players walked in. Zeke, Jason and Chad were the first ones to arrive. Zeke looked concerned.

"What's going on?" he asked. "Is the recipe okay? How are the cupcakes looking?"

Taylor explained the situation. Zeke nodded and took it all in. He surveyed the kitchen and then started giving orders to the team.

Gabriella was amazed at how quickly the boys got into formation and did what Zeke asked. All those drills made them really responsive! They were quick on their feet and followed directions. Gabriella could tell that even Taylor was impressed.

There was a knock on the kitchen door, and Gabriella peered through the curtain to see who was there. Martha and Timothy were standing by the door holding a couple of supermarket bags in their arms. When they walked into the bustling kitchen, they looked surprised to see the scene. They had only left about 30 minutes ago and at that point Gabriella and Taylor were still cleaning up after the batter incident. Now, the kitchen had a totally different feel. A larger team was in place, and there was a sense of calm.

"Wow," Timothy said as he evaluated the situation in the kitchen. "With these new parameters, I've recalculated – and we can make it!"

Martha put her bags up on the counter. "Now we can seriously rock out those orders!"

Taylor started to unpack the bags. She handed Chad and Jason a box of sugar so they could mix the icing.

"When do I get to lick the bowl?" Chad asked. Then he winked at Taylor. "Though I bet it isn't as sweet as you!"

Taylor rolled her eyes. Then she handed another box to Chad.

"Thank you, my dear," Chad said in a thick British accent.

"Oh, please," Taylor muttered. Then she moved on to the batter boys to give them more flour. But she did look back at Chad and give him a small smile.

Zeke tapped a wooden spoon to a metal bowl

to quieten the room. He took a cupcake in his hand. "Okay, here's the drill," he said. "They're the same principles involved in playing basketball. You go in for the layup by holding the cupcake up in front of you. Then you take a spoonful of icing, swoop it down the court–"

Zeke took a spoonful of icing and plopped it on top of the cupcake. "–and then you swish." He spread the icing with the back of the spoon. "Score!" he exclaimed as he held up a perfectly iced cupcake.

"Then you bring it over to this station and it gets a sprinkling of red decorations." He walked near the sink to a plate full of sparkly red sugar balls. He pinched them between two fingers and let them fall gently on the white cupcake top. He held up the finished cupcake for the crowd.

There were some whoops and cheers.

"Nice work," Gabriella said.

Zeke smiled. Then he got everyone working. Chad and Jason seemed to really get into the swooping. They were icing all the cupcakes with a loud 'score'! when they finished off each one.

In the living room, Troy and Gabriella were boxing and labelling all the cupcakes. Each cupcake was put into a small box with a love note attached. Gabriella and Taylor had printed out the notes earlier so all that needed to be done was to attach the note to the box.

"I don't know how to thank you," Gabriella said to Troy when they were alone in the room. "Without your help, and the team's, we never would have pulled this off."

"Glad that we could help," Troy said. He looked down at the box he was holding and then back up at Gabriella. "I know that I have been practising a lot lately. I don't want you to think that I forgot about what this Friday is."

"I know," Gabriella said with a little smile. "It's the big game against the Tigers."

"No," Troy said. "It's Valentine's Day. Did you think I had forgotten?"

The doorbell rang, and Gabriella looked at Troy. "I should get that," she said and went to open the door. She wished that her conversation with Troy could keep going. Was it possible that he had been thinking about Valentine's Day all week, too?

The bell rang again before she could reach the door. Whoever was standing on the porch was not being very patient. When Gabriella opened the door, she was amazed at who she saw there.

"Hello, Gabriella," Sharpay said.

"Hey, Gabriella," Ryan echoed.

Gabriella was stunned. She couldn't believe that Sharpay and Ryan Evans were standing on her front porch. She was sure a mean comment was going to come from Sharpay. She braced herself.

"We heard that the Decathlon team's cupcakes have the potential to be a top-grossing performer for the Heart to Heart Challenge," Sharpay said. "And we heard that you are a little behind in the orders."

Gabriella was about to snap at Sharpay that things were much better now, but then she saw a smile spread across her face.

"We're here to help," Sharpay said.

"We're actually really good bakers," Ryan added.

Gabriella laughed. "Of course, you are!" Then she opened the door wider and let them inside. "How did you know that we needed help?"

"Oh, we know all," Sharpay said. "Especially when it comes to the Heart to Heart fundraiser."

The evening was turning out a little differently than Gabriella had expected. She showed the Evans siblings into the kitchen where Zeke was happy to see another two pairs of hands.

After just 30 minutes, the situation had drastically changed. The scene in the kitchen was calm and happy. Everyone seemed to be pulling together fast. Gabriella caught Troy's eye through the open door in the kitchen. He was still at the living room coffee table attaching the printed love notes. He caught her eye, and they shared a smile.

East High really does have heart, Gabriella thought. And Troy had remembered that Friday was Valentine's Day. She grabbed a wooden spoon and jumped in line to ice a cupcake.

CHAPTER NINE

Kelsi couldn't believe her eyes. East High was decked out in red-and-white streamers, and large banners hung in every hallway.

Good thing the school colours were red and white, she thought. The decorations not only served as pep-rally incentives, but also as tie-ins for Valentine's Day.

She walked to the cafetcria where she was supposed to meet Ryan and Sharpay right after registration. As she entered the room, Kelsi couldn't help but notice the largest heart that she'd ever seen mounted on the back wall of the cafeteria. Across the heart was a banner that read, EAST HIGH HAS HEART.

"It's spectacular, isn't it?"

Kelsi turned around to see Sharpay grinning at the oversized heart.

"Ryan and I put that up yesterday afternoon," Sharpay explained. "It really adds something, don't you think?"

"A lot of red," Kelsi answered honestly.

"Hmm, perhaps," Sharpay mused. "But I like it."

"Hello, ladies!" Ryan sang out as he entered the cafeteria. "Nice flowers, Sharpay." He pointed to the bouquet that his sister was holding close to her chest.

Sharpay blushed. "Thanks," she said.

"Oh, come on," Ryan said. "You don't have to pretend. It's just us. We know that you sent yourself flowers earlier this week to get everyone psyched up for the flower drive." He rolled his eyes at Kelsi. "Come on, that's the oldest trick in the book."

Sharpay smelled the flowers in her hand. "Well, that might be true, but I didn't send these to myself. They are from an admirer."

Ryan rolled his eyes. "Oh, please."

"Seriously," Sharpay said. "They're from Zeke. Isn't that sweet?" She held out the card from the bouquet so Ryan could read it.

"Wow," he said. "These *are* from Zeke." Then he looked at Kelsi. "Did you know about this?"

"Actually, I did," she said. She had to hand it to Zeke. He knew how to please the ladies.

"I know that you handled all the orders," Sharpay said to Kelsi. "But there is one that you didn't see." Sharpay nodded to Ryan, who then went into the cafeteria kitchen. When he returned he was holding a very large bouquet. He handed it to Kelsi.

"For me?" she asked.

"Yes," Sharpay said. "Thanks for all your hard work. Happy Valentine's Day, Kelsi."

Kelsi was speechless. It was the first time that she actually started to feel as if Valentine's Day wasn't so bad after all. "Thank you," she said.

Just then, Sharpay's mobile phone rang.

"Helloooo!" she sang. With her ear pressed to the phone, Sharpay's face changed drastically from a smile to a grimace. "Yes, happy Valentine's Day to you, Hilary."

Ryan rolled his eyes and then tried to move closer to hear what the West High princess had to say about her school's progress.

"We're all fine here, thank you," Sharpay said into the phone. Then she made a face to Ryan and Kelsi. "Yes, for sure. Okay, we'll talk then. Bye."

She quickly ended the call. "So sweet of her to call, huh?" Sharpay asked. "I can't wait until tonight when the tally is revealed."

"Just remember that the idea was to raise money," Kelsi said. "And we did do that."

"True," Sharpay said. "But I would love East High to win this challenge."

"Maybe we did . . ." Ryan said. "But maybe we didn't. Best not to get too worked up just yet."

"I know," Sharpay said. "How will we be able to wait the whole day?"

"Well, we've waited the whole week already," Kelsi reminded her.

"Hey guys!" Taylor called from across the room.

As Taylor walked over to them, she did a double take at the extra-large heart hanging on the wall. When did that get there? she wondered.

When she reached Sharpay, she burst out with her news. "I just wanted to tell you that every one of the cupcake orders was filled and delivered this morning!"

"That's great!" Ryan said, clapping his hands.

Sharpay flipped some pages on her clipboard and made a few notations. "Yes, excellent." Then she took a deep breath. "Principal Matsui will announce our tally during half-time at the game tonight."

"The basketball team has their fundraiser this afternoon," Taylor said. "And they're still collecting pledges."

"That pep rally is going to be jumping," Kelsi said with a smirk. She loved a good pun.

Gabriella stood near the gymnasium doors as the bell rang for the end of seventh period. She had planned on meeting Troy there before the pep rally began. As Gabriella watched people head in to find seats in the stands, she couldn't help but feel the school spirit circulating in the halls. She smiled . . . that same school spirit was what helped get all those cupcake orders filled the previous night.

"Hey!" Troy called. He was decked out in his Wildcat red-and-white basketball warm-ups and appeared from one of the side doors.

"Hi," Gabriella said. "Nice that the school colours match the day's events, huh?"

Troy smiled. "Well, you know that we Wildcats have heart."

"Cute," Gabriella said. It was nice being able to kid around with Troy again. Actually, just being able to talk to him was nice! This past week had been a little out of the ordinary for them.

"Thanks for the flowers this morning," Gabriella told him.

"You're welcome," Troy said. Then he reached into his jacket pocket. "Here, I have something else for you." He handed her a small, beautifully wrapped box.

Gabriella couldn't stop smiling. She took the box and held it in her hands. It was perfect, with bright, shiny, red wrapping paper and a soft, white bow. *He did remember* was the thought that kept running through her head.

"Open it," Troy said. He was getting a little impatient. He shuffled his feet and seemed a little jumpy. "We only have a few minutes."

"Thank you," she said as she carefully unwrapped the gift. She gently lifted the top up and then pulled out the heavy piece of cotton wool stuffed in the box. Inside was a silver charm bracelet. She lifted it out and admired the piece of jewellery.

"See, there's a heart and a basketball," Troy said as he pointed at the charms. "And a cupcake, too."

Gabriella grinned. "This is the best Valentine's gift ever," she exclaimed. "I love it! It will always remind me of this Valentine's Day."

Then she reached into her backpack and took out a box for him. Troy looked surprised to see that she had got him a gift as well.

"I didn't know what I should get you," Gabriella explained. "And then with all the cupcake orders, I didn't really have a lot of time. But, well, here it is."

Troy took the box and opened up the gift. "A basketball cupcake! It's perfect!"

Gabriella was happy. Troy looked very touched. And she had to admit that the special cupcake had come out pretty well. It was a round ball that she had iced to look like a basketball. She had decorated the cupcake holder to look like a net and had written WINNING SHOT across the middle.

"I'm impressed," Troy said. "And it looks good enough to eat!"

"Well, it's not Zeke's recipe," she confessed. "But it is my nana's, and her cupcakes are pretty good."

"Thanks, Gabriella," he said. "I love that you made this for me. Thank you."

"You're welcome," Gabriella replied. "I know that you've been busy, so I went ahead and made a plan for tonight. I thought it might be a fun surprise."

"Really?" Troy asked. "That's so great." He was smiling broadly. "I made a plan, too. There's this new café that has karaoke. What do you think?"

Gabriella started to laugh. "That's the same place that I was thinking about!"

"Then it must be the right place for us to go," Troy said.

"It will be a great place to celebrate a Wildcat

victory," she told him. At that moment the bell rang again. The last period of the day had finally arrived, and it was time for the East High pep rally.

"Are you ready?" Gabriella asked.

"I hope so," Troy said. "See you inside."

"Good luck!" Gabriella called.

Troy gave her a big smile. "Thanks!" And then he ducked through the gym doors to join the rest of the team. He went directly into the locker room to store his cupcake safely in his locker.

"Hey, Wildcats!" Chad called as he came into the locker room. "What's up?"

"Our score!" Zeke yelled as he slammed his locker shut. "Let's go Wildcats!"

There were lots of shouts and screams as the team got ready for the Big Jump.

Having this fundraiser as part of the pep rally was going to raise money – but it also would pump up the whole team. Troy was pleased with his idea. Now he just hoped that the team had gathered enough sponsors to put East High over the top.

Troy noticed that his dad was talking to Principal Matsui in the doorway of the Principal's office. He had a few minutes before his dad came over to address the team. As Captain, Troy wanted to say a few words to his team-mates.

"Hey, Wildcats!" Troy shouted. Then he waited for everyone to gather around. "I just want to thank you guys for last night. All the cupcake orders were filled," Troy told them. "And all the money was collected."

"Swoop, swish, score!" Jason yelled.

The team cheered.

"Now we just have to go out there and jump!" Troy said. "We have to show the school that we have the spirit and the heart to be champions!"

"Yo, ready to jump?" Chad screamed.

"You know it!" Troy answered. He ran to the wall where the skipping ropes were hanging on pegs. He picked one up and then looked back at the team. "Let's go jump up East High!"

CHAPTER TEN

The sounds from the gym were so loud that Coach Bolton had to scream in order for his team to hear him. He told them to huddle by the locker-room doors while they waited for the band's music cue to enter the gym.

"Man, I am so psyched," Chad said to Troy.

"I know," Troy said. "This is the day we've all worked for – all the long practices–"

"And all the drills!" Chad said, finishing Troy's sentence.

"Do you think that you are up for the Big Jump?" Troy asked.

"Oh, you know it!" Chad told him. "I've got to honour my pledges . . . and please my fans."

"And the girls you promised that you'd be jumping for!" Jason added.

The band started to play the school fight song, and the cheers from inside the gym got louder and louder.

When he heard the cue, Coach Bolton moved aside so that the team could run out to centre court. "Go out there and jump, Wildcats!" Coach yelled.

Troy was the last one in line, and his father grabbed his arm before he ran out.

"Son, this was a great idea," he said. "I am proud of how you are leading this team. Principal Matsui told me that you and the boys have been hustling those pledges. You are doing your part for East High — and getting in a last-minute drill before the big game! Good job!"

Troy grinned at his dad. "Thanks, Dad," he

said. Then he ran out to meet up with his team at centre court.

As soon as the crowd saw the players, the screams got louder and people started chanting, 'Wildcats'!

There was a microphone set up at centre court and Troy went right to it. He stood there and waited for the crowd to quieten down.

"Hey, Wildcats!" he said. "We're here to jump you up for the game!"

There were tons of screams and cheers. Troy looked at his team-mates. They all looked very happy.

"We appreciate all of your pledges and support," Troy told the crowd. "Now we are going to jump for a total of 30 minutes. We'll take turns in groups. And we'll jump throughout this pep rally."

The cheerleaders ran out holding large red hearts with each of the players' names printed on them. They lined up across the foul line, and the crowd gave a loud cheer.

"Thanks, Wildcats!" Troy yelled. "And come out to cheer for us tonight, too!"

He took a step back and got in line with Jason, Zeke and Chad. They were going to be the first jumping group. While they jumped, the twirlers did their routines, and the band played their songs.

Sharpay was sitting with Ryan. They were both watching closely. This was the loudest pep rally they could remember, and probably the only one where the school was raising money with their school spirit.

If only Hilary could see us now, Sharpay thought.

Taylor and Gabriella were sitting a few rows behind Sharpay and Ryan. They were standing and holding signs to cheer the basketball team on. They knew that it was much easier to keep jumping when you had a team of friends rooting for you.

The cheer squad was up next. Everyone was pulling out all the stops for this pep rally.

After the last shake of the pom-poms, Principal Matsui went to the microphone. He pointed to the clock.

"We're almost at the halfway point!" he said. "Let's keep these players going. This is hard work!" Then he took a skipping rope from his pocket and he did a few jumps himself.

The crowd went wild.

Ms Darbus was so inspired that she, too, grabbed a skipping rope and began to jump. And then Coach Bolton did the same.

The basketball team's energy got a huge boost. And the crowd began chanting, "Wildcats got heart!"

Troy spotted Gabriella in the crowd. She held her sign up higher so that he could read it. JUMP IF YOU'VE GOT HEART, the sign said. Troy smiled and kept on jumping.

The crowd began to count down the final minutes of the 30-minute pep rally. A loud buzzer rang out over the sound system, and the team put down their skipping ropes.

The Big Jump was over!

"Thanks to all the players," Principal Matsui said, standing at the microphone. "We will see you all here tonight for the game against the Tigers!"

"Go home, rest and eat a good dinner," Coach Bolton advised the team as he hustled them back into the locker room. "We'll see you here tonight for the game."

"I'm getting used to that sound," Chad said as the team gathered around the locker-room doors later that evening. They could hear the noise from the crowd gathered in the gym. "We have some pretty decent fans."

"Yes," Coach Bolton said. "But you've got to keep your head in the game. Don't be distracted. The Tigers are a good team. Remember defence, and keep your eyes on the ball."

"Go Wildcats!" Troy yelled.

The team was ready. They had practised hard and trained for this game all season.

"Let's go!" Coach cried, hustling the team towards the court.

When Troy ran out he searched the crowd. Gabriella was right at the front. She was sitting with the Decathlon team. They were all on their feet, cheering.

The game started with a basket from Zeke and then one from Jason. All was going well. But the Tigers were a fast team, and they had a strong attack. By half-time, the score was tied.

Coach Bolton addressed the team in the locker room. "Team, this week has been all about heart." He looked around at all the players. "You guys showed what kind of hearts you have during the pep-rally fundraiser. And I was very proud. All we need to do is bring just a little bit of that heart out on the court in the second half, and the Tigers won't stand a chance! Go Wildcats! Let's go get 'em!"

The team roared and ran back out to the crowd. They arrived in the gym just as the Principal took the microphone in his hands.

"Wildcats," he said, "I have the grand tally of East High's Heart to Heart Challenge."

The crowd went very quiet. Everyone wanted to hear the news. Sharpay looked over at Hilary and her West High friends. They were eager to hear the announcement as well.

"Thank you for your attention," Principal Matsui said. He took a deep breath, drawing out the quiet moment a little longer. "I am proud to say that East High raised the most money in the history of this school – and has won the Heart to Heart Challenge!"

Sharpay leaped out of the stand and went running up to Principal Matsui. She hugged him while she continued to jump up and down.

"Omigosh, omigosh!" she cried. "We did it!"

She grabbed the microphone. "East High," she said as she continued to hold on to the Principal and jump, pulling him up and down along with her. "Thank you! You are all the best!"

Principal Matsui seemed a bit uncomfortable jumping up and down with Sharpay in the middle of the gym. He tried to calm her down. Then he motioned for Ryan to come over. Ryan took hold of his sister's hands and began to jump with her instead. Principal Matsui gently moved them to the side.

"Okay, East High," the Principal said, slightly out of breath. "Now, let's hear it for our basketball team. The score is tied, and they need to hear you cheer!"

The buzzer sounded, and the players were back in the game. Both teams were playing their best. The ball was moving quickly up and down the court.

Gabriella was biting her nails. The score was still tied. Each time the Wildcats scored, the Tigers countered with a basket of their own. The teams were a good match, and they kept trading the lead back and forth.

The roar of the crowd kept getting louder. As the minutes ticked away, the crowd got on its feet. Everyone was screaming. And then the Tigers scored two baskets in a row.

Troy looked to the sidelines. His dad was motioning for him to go down the court. Troy took the ball and tried for a basket. A tall Tiger tried to steal the ball, and the whistle blew. The ref signalled for two foul shots. Troy stood on the free-throw line. The crowd went crazy.

Bouncing the ball, Troy looked up at the basket. He had made hundreds of these shots all week at practice. He just had to make two. He held the ball up and let it go. *Swish!* One point. The gymnasium erupted in cheers. The ref threw the ball back to Troy. Again, he bounced the ball, concentrating. He released the ball up and held his breath as it went in. Now the Wildcats were only down by two.

The Wildcats were lucky enough to get the ball back quickly. There were just 16 seconds left on the clock. Troy knew that he had to go for a three-point shot. Scanning the court, Troy looked for one of his team-mates. They were all being guarded, so he took the ball down centre court himself.

Come on, he thought. Give me an opening. He glanced up at the clock. There were only 14 seconds left.

Chad waved his arms and Troy sent the ball straight to his chest, just as he had a hundred times during drills. It was a good pass, and Chad dribbled the ball closer to the net. But a tall Tiger was doing a great job of guarding him. Chad looked back at Troy. He had to give the ball back to him if they were going to attempt a basket.

Troy grabbed the pass from Chad, quickly moving away from the Tiger covering him. There were only two seconds left. He saw an opening, jumped, and let the ball take off from his finger-tips. The ball arched over the other player's fingers. For Troy, the ball seemed to be moving in slow motion.

The buzzer sounded.

The ball hit the rim and then touched the backboard. Then it rolled into the basket for three points! East High had won the game!

Troy was swept up by his team-mates. They

raised him up and carried him around the court. Troy saw his dad hugging Principal Matsui. Then he saw Gabriella rejoicing with the rest of East High.

Gabriella looked up and saw Troy. She waved and gave him a huge smile. This week could not have ended any better, she thought. Winning the Heart to Heart Challenge, and then Troy sinking the winning basket . . . East High did have heart. And Gabriella thought her heart couldn't get any fuller.

Troy screamed and ran to hug his team-mates. Then he raced over to Gabriella.

"Congratulations!" she shouted. "Great game!"

"Thanks," Troy said. "Are you still up for karaoke, Valentine?"

"Perfect," Gabriella told him.

"Where are we going after the game?" Chad screamed to Troy.

Troy looked over at Gabriella. He didn't know what to say. He wanted to celebrate Valentine's

Day with Gabriella, but he also wanted to celebrate the victory with his team.

Gabriella smiled. "We're all going to a karaoke café!"

Troy gave Gabriella a look. "Are you sure?"

"Yes," Gabriella said. "This Valentine's Day is all about teamwork. We have to celebrate with everyone tonight. As long as you promise to be my date."

Troy grinned. "And your valentine!" Then he turned to the stands and looked out at all the fans. "Wildcats got heart!"

Something new is on the way!
Look for the next book in the High School
Musical: Stories from East High series . . .

FRIENDS 4 EVER?

By Catherine Hapka
Based on the Disney Channel Original Movie
High School Musical, written by Peter Barsocchini

"**G**abriella Montez! Just the student I wanted to see!"

Gabriella stopped shuffling through the papers in her chemistry notebook and looked up. She had a quiz that day, and she wanted to make sure she had her notes so she could do a little extra cramming during registration. Gabriella had never received anything less than an A on a chemistry quiz in her life, but she didn't want to take any chances.

The Principal of East High was smiling at her from behind his wire-rimmed glasses. Beside him was a tall girl with strawberry-blonde hair and freckles. Gabriella had never seen her before.

"Hi, Principal Matsui," Gabriella said, closing her locker. "What's up?"

The Principal waved a hand at the tall girl. "Gabriella Montez, this is Ashley Appleton," he said. "She has just moved here from Michigan."

"Oh! Hi, Ashley. Welcome to East High." Gabriella smiled warmly at the girl. She had been the new girl plenty of times in her life, and she knew exactly how unnerving it could be to face a whole school full of strangers.

"Thanks," Ashley said. "It seems pretty cool here so far."

"Yes, yes." Principal Matsui rubbed his hands together. "I'm sure you'll find East High very, er, cool, Ashley. Gabriella is in your form, so I thought perhaps she wouldn't mind showing you around today." He smiled at Gabriella. "Ms Montez was the new girl in school herself not too long ago, so I know she'll treat you right."

"Sure," Gabriella said. "I'd be happy to show you around, Ashley. Did anyone show you how to work the lockers yet?"

"Not yet." Ashley giggled. "I just hope they're easier to open than the ones at my last school. I locked my favourite sweater in there for almost two weeks once. It was a total nightmare."

Principal Matsui checked his watch. "Better hurry, girls," he said. "The bell rings in 15 minutes."

He hurried off towards his office. Gabriella turned in the opposite direction and led the way down the hall. "It's too bad you had to switch schools in the middle of the term, Ashley," she said sympathetically. "That's really hard."

"Tell me about it!" Ashley rolled her eyes. "My dad's company was so totally useless about getting us here that I couldn't even convince him to let me stay in Michigan an extra two weeks for my friend Samantha's birthday ski trip. It's probably going to be the party of the century, and I have to miss it!"

Gabriella had never been all that interested in parties – or skiing, for that matter. But she understood how Ashley must be feeling.

"I know what you mean," she said. "When my mum got transferred from Illinois to San Diego, we had to move right before I was supposed to go on this really cool field trip to the science museum in Chicago. Oh! And the move before that?" She grimaced at the memory. "That one happened two weeks before my birthday."

Ashley shot her a curious look. "Whoa, it sounds like you've moved almost as much as me!"

"Eight schools in eleven-and-a-half years." Gabriella smiled ruefully.

"Only five schools here." Ashley laughed and held up both hands. "You win!"

Gabriella laughed. "Trust me, that's one award I'd love to give back! Still, it wasn't so bad.

At least I ended up here at East High. You're going to love it here – it's a really great school." She checked her watch. "We'd better hurry. The bell's going to ring soon."

EAST HIGH GUYS

(ACCORDING TO SHARPAY)

So you want to know about East High Guys? That's easy they fall into three distinct categories:

THE BALL GUYS

These guys spend their spare time chasing around after a ball of some description. They often have a misplaced sense of humour and absolutely no appreciation of the finer things in life, such as music and theatre.

THE BRAINIACS

These guys are usually members of the Chem Club or the Debabting Society. They like to hang out in the fusty old library or the smelly science lab and, although I can't prove anything, I think they probably all sing off key and have absolutely no sense of rhythm.

THE PRIMO BOYS

Sadly, these are a very rare breed at East High. They tend to appreciate culture and have a little more than sport filling their heads. The ultimate Primo Boy is of course Troy Bolton. Cultured, talented, good-looking and taken — but maybe not for long!

BALL GUY

PRIMO BOY

MEET THE BOYS!

This is the ultimate guide to East High's hottest hotties. Check out their style and their looks and get the low-down on what makes them so TOTALLY SWOONY!

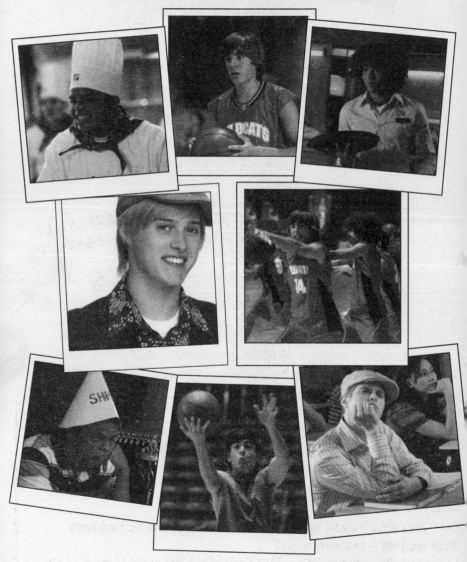

TROY BOLTON

Swoon city!

LAID-BACK, BLONDISH HAIR

INFECTIOUS SMILE

CASUAL BUT TRENDY JEANS-AND-T-SHIRT STYLE

ATHLETIC BODY (FROM ALL THOSE BASKETBALL DRILLS)

FACTS & STATS

Personality: FRIENDLY, CARING, DOWN-TO-EARTH

Best quality: A GREAT LEADER – UNANIMOUSLY VOTED WILDCATS CAPTAIN BY HIS TEAM.

Swoon factors: AMAZING BASKETBALL PLAYER, HEART-STOPPING SINGER

Hottie rating: 110% PURE HOTTIE!

QUOTES

CHAD 'He's a great leader and motivator, he's always there for his friends. What can I say – he's quite a guy!'

GABRIELLA 'He's got a really sensitive side and he's not afraid to stand out from the crowd. That's what makes him special.'

CHAD DANFORTH

One cool cookie!

CRAZY-COOL AFRO HAIR

★ AMAZING ★
DEEP-BROWN EYES

★ CHEEKY SMILE ★

FUNKY T-SHIRT-AND-TRAINERS STYLE

FACTS & STATS
Personality: FUNNY, BUBBLY, LAID-BACK
Best qualities: LOYAL – HE WOULD DO ANYTHING FOR THE TEAM AND THE GUYS
Swoon factors: SUPER- FIT BASKETBALL ACE, GREAT SENSE OF HUMOUR
Hottie rating: RED HOT!
QUOTES
TROY 'Chad never let's life get to him – he'll always crack a joke and lighten the mood. That's why he's such a good friend.'
TAYLOR 'He doesn't show his sensitive side very often, but when you get to know him he is such a loveable guy.

RYAN EVANS

A hottie with hats!

TRADEMARK HEADWEAR

BOYISH GOOD LOOKS

★ DAZZLING SMILE

FACTS & STATS

Personality: DRAMATIC. INDIVIDUAL

Best qualities: ENTHUSIASM – WHEN RYAN TAKES SOMETHING ON. HE REALLY THROWS HIMSELF INTO IT.

Swoon factors: INCREDIBLE SINGER AND PERFORMER

Hottie rating: STAR QUALITY!

SMART AND STYLISH DRESSER

ZEKE BAYLOR

What a sweetie!

★ A SMILE TO ★ MAKE YOU MELT

★ SPORTY/CASUAL ★ STYLE

FACTS & STATS

Personality: EASY-GOING. GENEROUS. PERFECTIONIST

Best qualities: INDIVIDUAL – ZEKE WASN'T EMBARRASSED TO ADMIT HIS LOVE OF BAKING TO HIS BASKETBALL GANG.

Swoon factors: WHO CAN RESIST A MAN WHO CAN COOK?!

Hottie rating: GOOD ENOUGH TO EAT!

CUTE. FRIENDLY FACE

LOVE MATCHES

Check out East High's hottest couples and find out what makes them so good together!

 TROY AND GABRIELLA

HIM	HER
Loves: KARAOKE	**Loves:** ANY KIND OF SINGING
Main interests: BASKETBALL AND SPORTS	**Main interests:** SCIENCE
Attitude: HARD-WORKING. FOCUSSED	**Attitude:** HARD-WORKING. FOCUSSED
Relationship style: SENSITIVE. ROMANTIC	**Relationship style:** ROMANTIC. CARING
In a word: RELIABLE	**In a word:** DEPENDABLE

THE VERDICT:
PERFECT HARMONY

Despite coming from different cliques at East High, these two are definitely singing from the same choir book. Their outlook on life is similar, they love helping and motivating others and they are there for each other 100%. The only problem they have is fitting some quality T and G time into their busy schedules!

 CHAD AND TAYLOR

HIM	HER
Loves: BASKETBALL	**Loves:** STUDYING
Main interests: BASKETBALL AGAIN	**Main interests:** CHEMISTRY AND GENERAL KNOWLEDGE
Attitude: DOESN'T TAKE LIFE TO SERIOUSLY	**Attitude:** HARD-WORKING. COMMITTED
Relationship style: LAYED-BACK	**Relationship style:** ROMANTIC. INTENSE
In a word: A JOKER	**In a word:** ACHIEVER

THE VERDICT:
OPPOSITES ATTRACT

It seems like these two have absolutely nothing in common, but that chalk and cheese combo seems to work. They have a tempestuous relationship, with lots of friction and quite a few tiffs, but they always work it out in the end, and when they make up they are stronger than ever before.

LOVE DESTINY

Maths doesn't have to be boring! Do some cosmic number crunching to find out some cool stuff about your personality, then do the Hottie Maths to find out which East High hunk could be your perfect match!

COSMIC CODE

1. **Take the number of your birth month (January is 1)**
2. **Add on your birthday**
3. **Add on the year (1994 is 1+9+9+4 = 23).**
4. **Now add it all up until you have one number:**

e.g. 1 + 15 + 23 = 39   3+9 = 12   1+2 = 3

WRITE YOUR NUMBER HERE:

HOTTIE MATHS

Step 1: WRITE YOUR CRUSH'S NAME IN THIS PANEL

Step 2: LOOK AT THE CHART BELOW AND WRITE DOWN EACH NUMBER THAT CORRESPONDS WITH EACH LETTER IN HIS NAME. ZEKE WOULD BE
8+5+2+5.

1	2	3	4	5	6	7	8	9
A	B	C	D	E	F	G	H	I
J	K	L	M	N	O	P	Q	R
S	T	U	V	W	X	Y	Z	

Step 3: ADD THE NUMBERS TOGETHER. ZEKE'S NUMBERS WOULD ADD UP TO 20. IF IT'S A TWO DIGIT NUMBER ADD THOSE TWO NUMBERS TOGETHER: 2+0 = 2.

WRITE YOU CRUSH'S NUMBER HERE:

Now, consult the Numbers of Destiny to see what sort of personality you and your crush have.

★ NUMBERS OF DESTINY ★

1= independent and ambitious

2 = generous and loyal

3 = a go-getter

4 = super-talented

5 = cool and adventurous

6 = sweet and down-to-earth

7 = fun-loving and layed-back

8 = meets challenges head-on

9 = hardworking and determined

COMPATIBLE NUMBERS

1 and 8

3 and 9

2 and 6

4 and 5

5 and 7

If you get the same number as your crush you are ultra-compatible!

LOCKER ROOM SECRETS

For girls, the East High locker room is shrouded in mystery (a bit like the girls washroom is for the boys). Taylor and Gabriella can often be found waiting for their freshly-showered men to emerge. But what really goes on in those off-limits locker rooms?!

MALE BONDING

As you probably suspected, the chat isn't just about shooting hoops. This is quality guy time where plans are made, secrets are revealed and conflicts are sorted. When it became obvious that Chad was more than a bit interested in one of the Brainiacs, the guys soon got the truth about Taylor out of him. And whenever Troy is off his game, the Wildcats know that it probably has something to do with Gabriella.

PROBLEMS SHARED

If Troy has got something on his mind — which is quite a lot of the time being such a sensitive guy — he knows that he'll get his friends full attention and (sometimes) helpful advice in the locker room. If he's torn between spending time with Gabriella and hanging with the Cats, the guys usually help him come to a decision — just not usually the right one!

COACH'S HEART-TO-HEART

Coach Bolton has a one-track mind when it comes to getting the team in shape, but once the whistle has blown for the end of the game he suddenly changes into the Wildcats' agony aunt. The guys can talk to him about anything, from their worries about the future, to their bad grades – and of course their shooting technique!

STEAMY SECRETS!

- WORD IS OUT THAT TROY SINGS IN THE SHOWER – ESPECIALLY AFTER A BIG WIN!
- RUMOUR HAS IT THAT CHAD HAS A LUCKY WILDCATS TOP THAT HE KEEPS FOR BIG MATCHES.
- ZEKE TRIES OUT ALL HIS NEW COOKIE RECIPES ON THE GUYS FIRST OF ALL – AFTER PRACTICE WHEN THEY'RE EXTRA HUNGRY.

♡ DREAM DATES ♡

Imagine you're a student at East High and you've got the chance to go out with an HSM hottie. Take the quiz and find out who your dream date would be!

1. When you go out for dinner, what is your favourite venue?
a) SOMEWHERE UPMARKET WITH SMART WAITERS AND FANCY FOOD
b) SOMEWHERE LAID-BACK AND RELAXED WHERE YOU DON'T NEED TO DRESS UP.
c) SOMEWHERE WITH SOFT LIGHTING AND MUSIC TO SET THE MOOD.
d) YOU DON'T REALLY HAVE TIME TO EAT OUT MUCH AS YOU'RE USUALLY STUDYING.

2. What sort of music do you like to listen to?
a) YOU HAVE A SOFT SPOT FOR FILM AND MUSICAL SOUNDTRACKS.
b) SOULFUL SOUNDS WITH A KICKING BEAT.
c) YOU'RE UP FOR ANY KIND OF MUSIC SO LONG AS YOU CAN SING ALONG.
d) CLASSICAL OR EASY LISTENING – SOMETHING TO HELP YOU CONCENTRATE.

3. What is your favourite food?
a) SUSHI – MINIMAL. AND DRAMATIC.
b) NOTHING FANCY – BURGER AND CHIPS WITH ALL THE TOPPINGS.
c) PIZZA – YOU LOVE FOOD YOU CAN EAT WITH YOUR FINGERS.
d) FISH AND MORE FISH – GOOD BRAIN FOOD.

4. When you go to the cinema, what's your favourite sort of film?
a) SOMETHING WITH AN ALL-STAR CAST AND GOOD MUSIC. LIKE MOULIN ROUGE.
b) AN ACTION MOVIE – LOTS OF EXCITEMENT AND CAR CHASES.
c) LOVE STORIES. COSTUME DRAMAS AND TRUE STORIES.
d) HISTORICAL EPICS OR DOCUMENTARIES.

5. When you're chatting with your mates, what do you often end up talking about?

a) CELEBRITY GOSSIP AND THE LATEST FASHIONS.
b) YOU JUST JOKE AROUND AND HAVE A LAUGH.
c) PERSONAL STUFF - BOYS. PROBLEMS.
d) WHAT'S IN THE NEWS. GOOD BOOKS YOU'VE READ.

6. What do you wear for a date?

a) SOMETHING WITH THE WOW FACTOR THAT MAKES YOU REALLY STAND OUT.
b) SOMETHING CASUAL - NICE JEANS AND A T-SHIRT.
c) SOMETHING THAT MAKES YOU FEEL GIRLY AND PRETTY.
d) SOMETHING QUITE DRESSY.

7. How long do you spend getting ready?

a) 2HRS - 1 HR IN THE BATHROOM AND 1HR CHOOSING WHAT TO WEAR.
b) WHAT DO YOU MEAN 'GET READY'?
c) DEPENDS - COULD BE 10 MINUTES COULD BE 10 DAYS!
d) PRECISELY HALF AND HOUR.

8. What's your bedroom like?

a) BUSY AND COLOURFUL - SHOES. HATS. POSTERS. CUSHIONS EVERYWHERE!
b) CHAOTIC BUT COMFY.
c) A HAVEN - FULL OF PHOTOS AND MEMORABILIA.
d) NEAT AND STUDIOUS - EVERYTHING PUT AWAY IN ITS PLACE.

9. What do you never leave home without?

a) A MOBILE PHONE - YOU HAVE TO BE CONTACTABLE AT ALL TIMES.
b) YOUR WATCH - YOU HATE NOT KNOWING WHAT THE TIME IS.
c) YOUR DIARY - YOU HAVE SO MANY COMMITMENTS IT'S EASY TO LOSE TRACK.
d) A GOOD BOOK OR SOMETHING INTERESTING TO READ.

10. What impresses you most in a guy?

a) HIS AMAZING STYLE
b) HIS SENSE OF HUMOUR
c) HIS WARM PERSONALITY
d) HIS INTELLIGENCE

YOUR SCORES

As	Bs	Cs	Ds

 YOUR DATE

Mostly As – RYAN EVANS

You and Ryan would get on like a house on fire. You both love looking good, dressing up for big occasions and making dramatic statements. Your date together would probably be upmarket sushi followed by front row seats at a musical.

Mostly Bs – CHAD DANFORTH

You and Chad are both cool, laid-back and up for a laugh. You're not into making too much effort or doing anything fancy. On your date together you would probably go to the cinema (or a basketball game if you were up for it) and then grab a burger somewhere cheap and cheerful.

Mostly Cs – TROY BOLTON

You and Troy are made for each other! You're both sensitive, romantic and sensible and you just enjoy hanging out and getting to know someone. On your date together you might have a picnic in the park followed by amoonlit walk – or a trip to a karaoke café!

Mostly Ds – A BRAINIAC

You would have a good time with any member of the chem club! You are intelligent, studious, serious and deep. You love reading, swapping amazing facts and broadening your mind. Your date might not be very romantic or exciting, but it would definitely be interesting, with plenty of lively conversation.